THE BEACH

LORNA DOUNAEVA

Copyright © 2024 by Lorna Dounaeva

All rights reserved.

No part of this book may be reproduced in any form or by any electronic or mechanical means, including information storage and retrieval systems, without written permission from the author, except for the use of brief quotations in a book review.

PROLOGUE

The sun beat down on the balcony. He shielded his eyes with his hand as he surveyed the empty pool below. He chugged his bottle of water and smiled as he thought about last night's party. One of the lads had got hold of some Rakia. That was the stuff the locals drank. They'd all downed it like it was water, and there was no one to tell them they'd had enough. He relished that freedom, even now, while he dealt with the brain ache.

It had been an epic night. They'd found a local radio station that was pumping out hardcore dance. People had heard the thumping base and come up to join them. The villa had been filled with sweaty bodies, swaying and grinding, well into the early hours. He had never danced with such abandon, never enjoyed such intense, stimulating conversation, never felt so understood.

This very balcony had been heaving. People had come out here to smoke and ended up getting off with each other indiscriminately. It had been wild.

He recalled those magical words whispered in his ear, as soft as the sand on the dunes:

'I've had enough of playing it cool. You drive me crazy. I think I'm falling for you.'

His lips tingled at the memory. He couldn't believe it. Was he in love? How could he be sure? He had never felt like this before.

He debated whether to join the others at the beach. He been neglecting them, caught up in his holiday romance. But his head was still sore. Perhaps it would be best to hang out here and wait for his…

He felt a sudden force against his back. He stumbled forward and tried to twist around to see who it was, but strong arms lifted him off the ground and tipped him upside down, holding him by his legs.

'Hey! Not funny!' he squealed. He was almost certain it was one of his mates, but the quiet was disconcerting. No talking, no laughing. Just utter silence as he was dangled mercilessly over the railings.

'Stop it! Let me up!'

Blood rushed to his head. He felt pressure in his ears and nose. He clawed the air in front of him, as he tried to find something to hang on to, but it was too late, he was being swung like a rope. The next thing he knew, he was flailing, falling through the air.

A scream erupted from his throat as he went down.

His body slammed against the water and the air left his lungs. A discordant note clanged in his ears, and his head felt like it was filled with static. His vision went black and fuzzy. He kicked his legs, trying not to panic at the tightness in his chest as he resurfaced, gasping for air. In the distance, he heard muffled voices. Someone would help him. He just had to tread water a little longer.

He did his best to keep his head up, fingers grasping, desperate to find the side of the pool, but his strength faded with every passing second, until the darkness swallowed him whole.

CHAPTER ONE
WILLOW

Saturday

Willow's hands quivered slightly as she dragged her tartan suitcase across the asphalt. She had waited for this day for so long. Planned for it and counted down to it. She held her breath as she passed the huddle of smokers outside the exit, taking their last frantic gasps of nicotine. The automatic doors whooshed open with a mechanical groan as she led the way into the airport.

Fluorescent lights blazed overhead, casting harsh reflections on the polished floor, while a symphony of announcements, footsteps, and rolling luggage reverberated off the sterile walls. She scanned the terminal and pointed her friends to the correct place to wait. Her brother Josh barged past her, heading directly for the check in desk.

'Josh!'

She thundered after him and tapped his shoulder.

'There's a queue!'

'Oh, I didn't realise.'

She shook her head, struggling to understand how he could not have noticed all those people.

They returned to where the others were standing and Tiana promptly pulled out her compact to check her eyelashes. She was the only one who did not look like they had just fallen out of bed. How she could be bothered to put on a full face of make up so early in the morning was beyond her.

She herself was fresh faced and so was Lia. Actually, Lia could really use a little make up. She looked pasty and dull. She bit her tongue and told herself not to be so mean. Lia was lovely. What did it matter what she looked like on the outside?

She glanced over at Hugo. At six feet tall, he towered over her, and yet with his stomping feet and stroppy expression, he reminded her of a toddler. Still, he was her brother's best friend so here she was, stuck with him for the entire week. He had better behave himself or she would make it her business to put him in his place. She did not suffer fools gladly.

Josh immediately struck up a conversation with a petite young woman. Willow couldn't hear what they were saying, but the girl was tipping her head back and laughing. This was nothing unusual. Her brother always had this effect on women. It was gross, the way they threw themselves at him. Of course, these random women had never seen his snotty nose when he had a cold, or the piles of toe-nail clippings he left on the side of the bath. They just saw white-blond hair and intense blue eyes and thought he was some kind of adonis.

That was just the way it was. Josh got the looks, Willow got the brains. Not that she was Einstein, but she had passed all her A-levels, which was more than could be said for him.

They moved forward in the queue, dragging their suitcases behind them. Hers wobbled a bit where one of the wheels was chipped. Behind her, Tiana and Lia were so busy talking they didn't even notice the queue had moved forward.

'Come on!' she called to them. 'Keep up.'

'I'm hungry,' Hugo moaned.

'We'll get food once we go through. Or on the plane.'

'I can't wait that long!' He looked back at the sandwich bar they had just passed.

'You need to stay in the queue.'

'I could nip out now. We've got time.'

'No, we're getting near the front.'

It was his own fault he hadn't eaten. They would have had plenty of time, but he had left his packing till the last minute and made them miss the first bus.

'I'll just go and...'

'Seriously, you need to wait.'

Hugo rolled his eyes. He had never respected her authority within the group. Even though she was the one who organised everything. A second checkout opened alongside the one they were waiting at and suddenly the queue was moving. She nudged her suitcase a few inches ahead, about to grab her phone, when a pair of hands clamped over her eyes. Her pulse spiked, adrenaline flooding her system. She whirled round, wild-eyed and breathless.

'Spence! What are you doing here?'

Spence grinned from ear to ear as if he had just pulled off a heist.

She clocked the bright blue Hawaiian shirt and sunglasses, the suitcase at his side, and inhaled deeply.

'Surprise! My boss gave me the week off!'

Everyone gathered around: Josh, Hugo, Lia and Tiana.

Tiana was the first to speak. 'Spence, you know we love you babes, but you can't just crash the holiday! You don't even have a plane ticket.'

'I just bought one! Last seat on the plane, apparently.'

Josh frowned. 'Where will you sleep?'

Spence smirked. 'I'm sure I can find room in your sister's bed.'

Josh shrugged. 'Up to you, mate. You do know she has chlamydia and rabies?'

He turned back to the girl he had been flirting with,

leaving Willow floundering like a crab on a dance floor. She imagined the ceiling splitting open and a flood of cold water pouring out. Spence looked so excited, but she had been planning this holiday for months, and he wasn't supposed to be a part of it.

And yet, here he was.

Lia's eyelids fluttered like frantic butterflies.

Tell him no. Tell him he can't come.

She looked at Spence again. His face was so open, so sincere. He really thought she would be happy. She *was* happy. She loved him. At least, she thought she did.

She drew a breath and when he pulled her into his arms, she didn't object. It would be fine. She just had to adapt. She would phone the restaurant and let them know there would be six people at Josh's birthday dinner, instead of five. And she would share her room with him instead of having it all to herself. She would make it work.

'I'm so happy.'

'You're sure?'

'Of course I am. It was just a bit of a shock, that's all.'

'A shock, or a surprise?'

'It's the same thing, isn't it?'

She breathed in his familiar scent and told herself to relax. She was getting a neck ache. She didn't want to be the first to pull away, but he was holding her a little too tight. Her jacket clung to her damp skin as sweat trickled down her back. She strained to see over his shoulder.

'The queue's moving forward.'

She ducked under his arm and grabbed her suitcase as they all shuffled up.

'Next please. Where are you going?'

Willow zoned in on a stern-looking woman whose round glasses seemed to take up half her face.

She pushed in front of her friends and handed over their

documents. Spence dropped his on top of the pile with a big grin.

'Burgas airport, Bulgaria.'

'How many of you are travelling?'

'Six.' She handed over their documents. Spence dropped his on top.

She flipped through them all, checking each face against the respective passport photo.

'Josh, stop bobbing about,' Willow said under her breath.

He looked directly at the officer and gave her an easy smile. To Willow's annoyance, her entire demeanour changed. A smile played on her lips and she ran a hand through her hair.

'And how many bags?'

'Six.'

'Seven,' the girl next to Josh corrected.

Willow narrowed her eyes.

The girl flicked a glance at Josh. 'He said he could put my extra one on his luggage allowance, because I'm probably over the limit.'

'Nope,' Willow said, shooting daggers at Josh. 'We're not taking your bag, sweetheart.'

Josh opened his mouth to object, but Willow overrode him.

'You don't know what might be in it.'

Josh hung his head. 'Sorry,' he said to the girl, who scowled.

They heaved their bags onto the conveyor belt and took their boarding passes and passports.

Willow rounded on her brother.

'I can't believe you were going to take that girl's bag. How naïve can you be?'

'She was harmless.'

'You don't know that. She could have had anything in that

bag. Drugs or whatever. You could have spent the next twenty years in prison.'

'I'm too pretty for prison.'

'I'm sure you'd be really popular.'

They headed for security and queued again to place their backpacks and iPads in trays. Everyone walked through the scanners and, amazingly, nobody set off the sensors. They were gathering up their stuff when one of the security officers came forward.

'Can you step aside a moment?' he asked Tiana.

'Me?' She looked pleased to be picked, as if it was an honour.

He pulled a big bag of cosmetics out of her backpack. 'What's all this?'

'VivaLux's summer skincare collection.'

His eyes narrowed. 'All liquids were supposed to be placed in a clear bag. No more than 100ml per person.'

Willow moved forward. 'I don't have any liquids. She can have my allocation.'

'And mine,' Josh said.

Quickly, they crammed the cosmetics into the required bags. There was clearly more than 100ml in each, but the security officer allowed it through, once it had all been scanned.

'He had really puffy eyes. Do you think I should give him a tube of wrinkle proof eye cream as a thank you?' Tiana murmured.

'I think you should keep your big mouth shut,' Willow said, shoving the last bag into Tiana's backpack. 'Come on. Let's get moving.'

They headed out of security. Spence stood in front of the departures board. 'We're boarding. Gate 56.'

Willow looked around. 'Wait, where's Hugo?'

'In the cafe.'

She turned and saw him standing at the counter. She felt her blood boil.

'There isn't time.'

'Try telling that to him.'

'He's already paid.'

Lia gave a little huff and flumped down on the floor. Tiana glanced furtively at Josh, who hadn't bothered to put his belt back on after security, and now his jeans were sliding down his bum. Hugo finally emerged, balancing a croissant dripping with melted cheese and a large takeaway coffee.

'Right, come on. We've got to go.'

Lia let out a groan as she hauled herself up and they set off towards the gate.

'Will you get a move on?' Willow hissed at Hugo, who had barely moved as he stopped to scarf down his breakfast.

Hugo blinked back at her with sheep eyes.

'Seriously! We're going to miss the plane.'

She felt tension in her jaw. She could have left him behind, but she didn't trust him to find his own way to the boarding gate.

She and Spence led the way, moving at a brisk pace as they headed down the corridor and onto the travelaters. They soon reached the end and stepped off, moving to one side as they saw that the rest of the party was way behind. Josh was somewhere in the middle, with Tiana right beside him, but neither Hugo nor Lia made any effort to move as the travelater squeaked along. Lia was reading the information posters on the walls while Hugo continued to stuff his face.

Spence placed a hand on Willow's shoulder. 'Just think of the beach,' he said, as they headed onward, along the corridor towards the gates. 'I can already see the shimmering aquamarine water. The white gold crystals of sand…'

An announcement rumbled out of the Tannoy and she distinctly heard their names.

'You hear that? That's the last call for our flight!'

They ran, even Lia, who was hot and sweaty from the effort. Still Hugo dawdled along behind them. She glanced back over her shoulder.

'Move it!'

'The coffee is burning my hand!'

'Dump it! We have to catch this flight!'

Spence sprinted ahead, his long legs speeding down the corridor.

She raced after him to the gate and stood there panting. The check in officer was dressed in a prim little uniform. Willow could see her own reflection in the buttons. Her hand shook as she held out the boarding cards.

'Boarding is closed.'

'Please let us through! I'm begging you!'

'I'm sorry, you're too late.'

CHAPTER TWO
WILLOW

Willow dabbed her temple. 'Our luggage is already checked in. Please, just let us on the flight.'

'The gate has closed.'

'I'm begging you!' Spence's eyes were welling up. 'We can't afford to buy more tickets.'

The check in officer barely glanced at them. Willow reached for Spence's hand and squeezed it. She couldn't believe her dream holiday was over. It was alright for Hugo. He could afford to miss planes, the posh twat. But there was no way the rest of them had the cash for more tickets.

Tiana and Josh appeared at her elbow.

'What's the matter?' Josh asked.

'They won't let us on.' She clenched her fists as anger tremored through her body.

Josh stepped forward, placing his hands on the counter. 'I'm really sorry we're late.'

At the sound of his deep baritone, the check in woman looked up from her terminal. Her eyes met his and she blinked, her pupils dilating slightly.

'Is there any way you could let us board? This is our first proper holiday. It will break my sister's heart if we miss it.'

'I…I'll ask the captain. That's all I can do.'

'Thank you. I appreciate it.'

She gazed at him a moment longer, then turned abruptly and headed for the jet bridge, her heels clicking against the floor as she disappeared from view.

Hugo and Lia rounded the corner. Lia was red faced and panting as she sank down in the nearest chair. Hugo was still eating his bloody croissant. He had got flaky pastry all down his shirt. He caught her looking at him and narrowed his eyes.

'What?'

'We're too late. They won't let us on the plane.'

'Sure they will.'

She fought the urge to scream. 'You really are the most entitled…'

'Willow!' Lia took her arm and pulled her to one side.

'What?'

'We need to stay calm. Fighting amongst ourselves won't get us anywhere.'

She glanced back at the jet bridge while Lia continued to drone on. Why was it taking so long? Were they offloading all their luggage?

Spence was scribbling furiously in his notebook.

'Are you seriously writing a poem right now?'

'I'm channelling my anxiety.'

'Breathe with me,' Lia said. 'In and out…'

She snarled as Hugo bit off another big chunk of his croissant. What wound her up the most was that he didn't even look flustered. She balled her hands into fists, fighting the urge to go over there and wallop him. Hugo had been annoying when they'd been in school together, scoring top marks in exams with very little effort on his part. And he had always been completely unflappable. But this, right now really took the biscuit.

She glanced over Spence's shoulder and saw that he had drawn a caricature of Hugo being crushed under the weight of a massive croissant. She felt her shoulders relax at the absurdity of it, and a surprised laugh burst out of her. Spence grinned, revealing the wide gap between his teeth. He had scribbled a verse to go with it, but it was the picture that did it for her.

The check in officer returned. She looked straight at Josh, as though he was the only person in the room.

'Please step this way. Quick as you can.'

Willow could have kissed her, but she didn't need to be asked twice. She glanced back at her friends, high-fiving Lia and Tiana. Hugging her brother. Then she grabbed her backpack and off they went.

She felt the glare of the other passengers, who were already seated as they made their way onboard. They slotted quickly into the last remaining seats and she shut her eyes, allowing herself a moment to breathe. She had worked so hard to get here. She deserved this.

CHAPTER THREE
WILLOW

'Taxi to Paradise Palms?' a man in a worn leather jacket said to Josh.

'Yeah, great.'

'No thanks, we already have transport,' Willow said, wrinkling her nose at the pungent smell of cigarettes. She waved the man away and leaned closer to her brother.

'He looked dodgy.'

'You think everyone's dodgy.'

'And you're too trusting by half.'

'Well, this bus of yours better turn up.'

'It will.'

The hot air swirled around them, carrying scents of the sea along with exhaust fumes from passing cars. In the distance, she could hear the sounds of street music interspersed with the cars honking and the wail of sirens. While they waited, Spence contorted his long limbs into a full on yoga pose. She fanned herself with the thriller she had picked up at the airport shop. Someone shoved past Tiana, causing her to drop her makeup bag, scattering lipsticks and mascaras all over the pavement. Lia helped her chase after them as they bounced and rolled into the bustling crowd. All the while,

The Beach

Hugo sat on a bench and spread out his newspaper, like an old man.

Willow wiped the sweat from her forehead and found that her hand was now covered in ink.

Where was the damned bus?

'Is that it?' Hugo asked, pointing to a bus that was waiting at the other end of the terminal.

'Yes, I think it is!'

Willow stuffed her book into her bag and helped Tiana gather up the last of her lipsticks. Spence unwound his limbs and sprinted towards it, leaving Willow to manage both their suitcases. The bus doors opened, and the driver helped load their cases onboard. They waited for a few minutes, but no one else got on, so it was just them on their own private bus to Paradise Palms.

They all looked out the windows as the bus trundled into the city and followed the coast road to the resort. Towering trees lined the route, the branches swaying gently in the warm sea breeze, casting shadows on the ground below. The sea appeared restless, churning with white caps and frothy foam. Rows of boats bobbed rhythmically with the ebb and flow of the tide; trawlers, sailing boats, and gleaming white yachts. And then there were the surfers out on the waves. They looked as though they had kites attached to their hands, giving them the ability to take off and fly through the air.

'Wow, look at that!'

'They're kite surfing,' Hugo said. 'I tried that last summer in Cornwall.'

They all watched as one of the riders went really high in the air, spinning and twisting before landing neatly, catching a wave back to the shore. The beach was the longest Willow had ever seen. It seemed to stretch out forever, miles of powdery white sand, just waiting for her.

The rusty old bus squealed to a halt.

'Final destination,' the driver said, in broken English. With a grunt, he got up from his seat and forced the doors apart.

'Thank you!' Willow said, stepping out into the heat of the searing sun. Two towering palm trees supported a crooked sign that creaked in the wind. It read:

'Welcome to Paradise Palms. You'll never want to leave.'

There were dozens of villas, grouped around a large swimming pool. The little office was empty, but Willow found the keys on a hook, as she had been instructed. Number seven was directly in front of them, the door slightly ajar. There was a strong smell of bleach as they entered, mingled with an older, muskier smell.

Inside, everything looked reasonably clean and tidy. A bowl of sweets had been placed on the counter, and for some reason, a man's shoe sat on top of the coffee table.

Tiana picked it up. 'Nice Italian leather,' she whistled, flinging it towards the door. They surged towards the bedrooms. Willow and Spence bagged the room at the back.

'Look, there's a little fridge!' She opened the door to find some soft drink cans inside. 'How lovely!'

Spence nodded. He was pushing the two single beds together to make a double.

'Oh look, we've got a balcony!' She ran out onto it and peered down into the pool below. The far end looked clear and shallow, but it grew gradually deeper and darker, until it became almost bottomless, like an endless abyss.

'Where is everyone?' Spence asked, wrapping his arms around her. 'I'd have thought it would be heaving.'

There were dozens of sun loungers set out with parasols, but there wasn't a soul to be found.

'They're probably all down on the beach.'

'Or perhaps they've found something better to do…' he nuzzled at her neck.

'I'm so hot and sweaty. I really want a swim.' She wriggled out of his arms and dug her new tartan bikini out of her suitcase. Shedding her clothes, she pulled it on, tying a long sarong around her middle. Then she packed a bag with a towel and sun cream, all the while Spence just stood there. She paused at the door and looked back at him.

'You coming or what?'

DOWN BY THE POOL, she saw a small kiosk. It was little more than a wooden shack, with a couple of plastic picnic tables outside. She walked up to the counter.

'Hi, can I have a lemonade please?' she pointed at the can she wanted, unsure whether she would be understood. She handed over a note and a woman who must have been around her mother's age passed her a couple of coins in change.

'Blagodarya,' she said, trying out the Bulgarian word for thank you.

The woman stared at her for a moment, then nodded. 'Thank you,' she said in perfect English.

Willow was going to say something more when Tiana appeared, wearing a gorgeous gold bikini that screamed, 'Look at me!'

She ordered herself a drink called Mastika, that smelled a bit like Ouzo.

'I can't wait to go out tonight,' Tiana said. 'Check out the clubs, have a little dance.'

'Yeah, it'll be great.'

She hoped Tiana's expectations weren't too high. There were only two clubs at the resort. And so far, they'd barely seen anyone. If she was hoping for a holiday romance, she might be disappointed.

Hugo and Josh wandered over and got themselves some beers.

'Oh, I forgot to text Mum! Unless you did?' Willow looked over at Josh.

'No.'

Of course not. These things always fell to her. Just because she was born eleven months before him. Or more accurately, because she was female.

'Try not to look drunk,' she warned Hugo.

'How am I supposed to do that?'

'You can put your tongue back in your head for a start. That's it, hold it like that.'

'Here, I'll take it,' Spence said, taking her phone.

Everyone crowded in together, Willow and Josh in the middle, Tiana squeezed in as close to Josh as she could get away with. Lia and Hugo crammed in on the end.

The photo was a good one, everyone smiling, looking happy. She tapped out a message to her mother:

'Having a lovely time. Wish you were here!'

She sent it off and sat back.

'Good thing you remembered, or she would be setting the police on us,' Josh said, reaching for his beer.

'Police? Now you're talking,' Tiana said with a sly smile.

They spent the afternoon in and out of the pool, getting drinks from the kiosk and playing dance music on their phones. In all that time, nobody else appeared, not even the club rep who was supposed to have been there to greet them.

At around five, they headed back to their villa and got dressed up for the evening. Tiana insisted on doing the girls' hair and make up, while the boys sat in the lounge, watching the football and drinking beer. When everyone was ready, they posed for more pictures, then Willow herded them all round the corner to a place called Mehana bar and grill.

'This is the place I booked for Josh's birthday,' she said.

The smell of sizzling meats and herbs wafted through the air as she peered inside. It had looked a lot more inviting on the website, with pictures of friendly staff serving platters of traditional food. In reality, the place was as empty as the rest of the resort. There was no one there, aside from an older couple by the window, who gawped at them as they looked around.

Willow heard faint voices and the clinking of utensils coming from the kitchen, but when a waiter finally appeared, he looked right through them and scurried by.

Willow looked at her friends uncertainly. 'Maybe people eat later here, you know. Like in Spain?'

'I'm not really hungry, anyway,' Tiana said. 'I want to party!'

They slipped out unnoticed and headed up the road, towards the bars. The first one was dimly lit and as empty as the restaurant had been. Not to be put off, Josh whipped out his wallet and bought them all shots.

'To the holiday of a lifetime!'

'What happens in Bulgaria, stays in Bulgaria,' Hugo chimed in.

Willow necked her drink and a warm buzz spread through her body. She waited impatiently for Lia to finish hers. Then they worked their way from bar to bar. The small night club at the end of the strip was closed, so they decided to trek up the steep hill to the larger one.

'My feet hurt,' Lia moaned.

'Climb on my back. I'll give you a piggyback,' Josh offered.

Lia whooped as he carried her up the hill. Tiana pursed her lips.

'My turn on the way back,' she said.

'You'll be carrying *him* on the way back,' Willow said. 'He's the world's biggest lightweight.'

'That could work too.'

They reached the top and Willow was relieved to hear music pumping out of the club. She could already feel the bass vibrating through her body. Two huge bouncers stood by the entrance, arms crossed, serious expressions on their faces. Willow gestured to Lia to hop down off Josh's back, then she walked up to them, flashing her ID. The bouncers waved them all in.

She headed inside and looked around. Bright pulsing lights cast patterns on the large dance floor, and the music was banging, but there were only about half a dozen people inside.

'Lucky us,' Willow said, brightly. 'We don't have to queue for everything and we get the whole dance floor. Who wants to dance?'

Tiana gave a whoop and she and Hugo stepped onto the dance floor.

Willow turned to the bar.

'The drinks are really cheap here,' Josh said

'I know, but let's not go nuts. We need to pace ourselves. It might be a good idea to have some water?'

Josh laughed and ordered himself another pint.

Spence grabbed her hand. His eyes simmered as he pulled her onto the dance floor. He moved with a natural ease, his body fluid and intoxicating. She let herself get lost in the music and the sensation of his hands on her hips.

A little later, three young women walked in. The one in the middle had incredibly long, jet black hair that fell past her waist in soft waves. She reminded Willow of a mermaid. The three of them perched daintily on bar stalls and watched the dance floor like hunters on the prowl. Their eyes flickered over Spence, Hugo and Josh and they smiled at each other, but they didn't stay long, only stopping for one drink before they headed out the door. She wandered where they were going onto. No doubt, there was a better, trendier club only the locals knew. She tried to voice this thought, but the DJ whacked up the music, and Spence couldn't hear her. She gave a careless shrug and continued to dance. Soon she was lost in the rhythm and the heat of the music. More people arrived just before midnight. Not just teens, but older people too. Most of the men wore leather jackets despite the heat, while the women wore as little as possible. The woman from the kiosk was there, dressed in a tank top and a short leather skirt. Willow tried to picture her own mother dressed this way and swallowed a laugh.

At around two in the morning, the music came to an abrupt end and the doormen promptly ushered them out. It was all over so fast, she barely had time to find her shoes, which she had kicked off at some point during the night.

By the time she had located them, everyone else had already left. Hand in hand, she and Spence walked back to the villa. The pool gleamed as they passed it, its surface shimmering like liquid silver. She heard a faint sound behind them and turned around, squinting into the darkness, but there was no one there.

'Wake up, Sleepyhead!'

Willow blinked and stared into the dim light.

'What time is it?'

'It's gone nine,' Spence said. 'We should be up. We've got some serious holidaying to do.'

'Why don't we just lie in?' she moaned.

'Because I've been awake since sunrise. Spectacular, it was. A burst of pinks and purples, like a little kid trying to paint with their fingers. Come on, I'm starving. Let's go and get something to eat.'

Willow hugged her pillow. It wasn't the comfiest bed. It was hard as a board, and the sheets were distinctly bobbly, but right at that moment, it felt like heaven.

'Five more minutes?'

'I'll buy you breakfast.'

Seeing he wasn't going to leave her alone, she wrenched herself out of bed and splashed water on her face. She could hear Tiana and Lia giggling in the room next door and felt a slight pang. Would she have had more fun with them?

When she came out of the bathroom, Spence seemed to

have forgotten his hunger. He wound himself around her body, kissing her all over.

'I haven't even had a shower yet,' she said.

'I don't mind.' He pulled her down on the bed and she couldn't be bothered to argue. She tried to relax her body as he did all the work, kissing her all over and using all his best moves to maximise her pleasure. But as she lay there, she found her mind wandering. Should she try to book a different restaurant for Josh's birthday, or should they try that place again? The food had smelled good. Perhaps they should try going later, like the locals?

'Oh, Willow!' Spence was gazing into her eyes and she forced herself to moan in response. Before she knew it, it was all over.

Spence rolled off her, satisfied. He lay there, gazing at her while she lay back in bed.

'I'm still hungry,' he said. 'Do you want to get some food?'

'Nah, I'd really like a lie in, if that's okay?'

'Worn you out, have I? Okay, I'll see you in a bit.'

He kissed her hand and headed out the door, leaving her in bed. It was nice to have the room to herself. Peaceful.

Tiana poked her head round the door.

'Lia's hogging the shower, so I thought I'd see what you were up to.'

'Just chilling out.'

'Where's Spence?'

'He went for breakfast.'

'You didn't want to go with him?'

'Not really.'

Tiana looked at her curiously. 'Are things alright between you too? I've been sensing a bit of a vibe lately, or am I imagining it?'

Willow shrugged. 'I don't know. I suppose this is what it's like when you've been together a while. We know each other backwards. There's no…novelty anymore. No excitement. Not for me at least.'

Tiana whistled. 'What are you saying?'

'I don't know. I mean, I do still have feelings for him, but I wish he had let me come on holiday on my own. It would have been good for us to have some time apart.'

'You wanted a chance to shag other men, you mean?'

'No, that's not it at all!'

'Isn't it?' Tiana walked towards the balcony. 'Hey, your view's way better than mine. You can see the whole pool.'

'Yeah, it's great.'

Her throat was as dry as sandpaper. She turned to open the little fridge. It had a weird smell that she didn't like to think about too much.

'I've got Fanta if you…'

She heard a yelp, and then a loud splash, and when she looked up, Tiana was gone.

CHAPTER FOUR
WILLOW

She ran to the balcony, immediately skidding on the greasy floor. She grabbed onto the thin railings and stared down into the pool below. There was a body in the water, completely submerged.

'Tiana!'

Carefully, she hurried back into her room, yelling to her friends,

'Help! Tiana's fallen off the balcony!'

Without waiting for a response, she burst through the door and charged round the side of the building. She saw Tiana broach the surface, splashing about, clearly disorientated.

'Tiana! I'm coming!'

She ran towards the pool and dived into the cool water, her flimsy dress billowing around her like an underwater parachute. Tiana thrashed about, clawing at her in desperation. The weight of her body dragged them both under, and Willow struggled to break free.

Tiana was still panicking, her arms wrapped tightly around her, preventing her from getting back up to the surface. Desperately, Willow tried to pull her away, but she had hold of a chunk of hair and it was impossible to loosen her grip.

Glancing up, she saw a bright orange object skimming the surface above them. She punched Tiana in the ribs, causing her to release her grip and she swam towards the object as fast as she could. Her hand found something firm and plastic and she wrenched herself up, gasping for air.

She heard someone shout and saw that the object she was holding onto was a life ring. Right at that moment, Tiana grabbed her again, grasping desperately at her legs. She really was drowning, Willow realised. She kept hold of the ring with one hand and used the other to pull her spluttering friend to the surface. Still in a panic, Tiana immediately clung to her neck.

'Over here!'

She looked up and saw the woman from the kiosk waving at her. She must have been the one to throw the life ring. She sucked down a long, deep breath and began kicking her way over. She saw that she was now holding out a long rod. As soon as she was close enough, Willow grabbed onto the end, and then they were being reeled in like fish.

When they reached the side, the woman bent down and hauled Tiana out of the water and onto the side of the pool. Tears sparked in her eyes as she hauled herself out, and turned her attention to Tiana, who lay on her side, coughing and spluttering.

She rubbed her friend's back, while the woman grabbed a beach towel and pulled it over her like a blanket. She handed one to Willow too.

'Thank you.'

Willow glanced at her, registering for the first time that she was the woman from the kiosk.

Tiana sat up, blinking in confusion.

'Are you alright? Do you want me to call an ambulance?'

She was already pulling out her phone when Tiana shook her head.

'No. No, please! I just need some water.'

She managed a weak smile, her head bowed as she caught her breath, breathing noisily in and out.

Willow leaned closer. 'Are you sure you're okay?'

'I think so.'

'What happened?'

'I'm not really sure. I stepped onto the balcony and skidded on something. The next thing I knew, I was flying through the air. It was fucking crazy.'

'Let's get you up onto a sun lounger, shall we?'

Tiana was still wobbly, so Willow helped her up and covered her with the towel. She looked terrible.

The kiosk lady came back with bottles of water for each of them, not taking her eyes off Tiana as she drank. Tiana wiped her mouth with her hand.

'I think we're alright now,' Willow said.

'I hope so, love.'

'You're English?'

'I should really introduce myself, shouldn't I? My name's Kelly. Kelly Armitage.'

It was a little disconcerting, the way she reached out and shook both their hands. Like they were at a formal dinner or something. The skin on her hands felt thin and crepey and her breath smelt like tobacco. Not cigarettes or vapes, but chewing tobacco, like the stuff her grandad smoked.

Kelly was still talking, but Willow didn't take in much of what she was saying. Tiana was unusually quiet too, still stunned by the accident.

'You probably want to change your clothes,' Kelly said.

Willow looked down at herself. Her dress was completely soaked, and a little see-through. She *should* go and change, but she didn't feel as though her legs would carry her, so she sat with Tiana a little longer. She was still concerned about her friend, who stared numbly out at the water, barely moving, barely saying anything.

Kelly got up and went back to the kiosk. A few minutes later, she returned with two cups of tea.

'Oh, thank you,' Willow said gratefully. 'Just what we needed.'

'It's going to get busier later. There's a coachload coming in from Romania.'

'Good to know.'

Willow looked around at the deserted pool. She would miss the peace and quiet, but the club nights could do with livening up a bit. She hoped there would be some hot guys for Tiana. She had been hung up on Josh for too long now, and who knew, maybe there would be someone for Lia too.

'What made you choose this place?' she asked Kelly.

The older woman had a distant look in her eyes. 'I came out here ten years ago and never went back.'

'Don't blame you,' she said, looking at the palm trees. All the same, it was hard to imagine living out here all year round, away from her friends and family. She guessed Kelly's life must not have been all that great back in England.

Kelly heaved herself to her feet. 'I'd better crack on. You give me a shout if you need anything, okay?'

'Thanks,' Willow said. 'And thank you for everything you've done. It's really good of you.'

'I'm just glad you're okay. Now sit there quietly, both of you. You've had a nasty shock. You need time to recover.'

Willow watched as she returned to the kiosk. What a nice woman!

'Have you seriously been swimming in your clothes?' Josh asked, walking down the path towards them.

'Tiana fell from the balcony.'

Josh's eyes flicked to Tiana. 'Are you okay?'

Tiana pressed her hand to her heart. 'I got the fright of my life. I could have drowned.'

'I saved her,' Willow said. 'Me and the woman from the kiosk.'

Josh didn't seem to hear her. 'You poor thing,' he said, enveloping Tiana in a hug. Tiana's expression was one of pure joy. She practically melted into his arms. They held that position for a moment until Hugo's voice exploded across the patio.

'Easy! What's going on here, then?'

Josh let go of Tiana.

'Tiana fell off the balcony,' Willow said.

Hugo's jaw dropped. 'What, right into the pool?'

He looked up at their villa and whistled. 'Hardcore!'

'It isn't funny. She could have drowned.'

'I don't know, looks like the ultimate diving board. Tell me you at least did a backflip?'

'It hurt when I hit the water. Major bellyflop. It knocked the wind out of me.'

'Well, I'm glad you're okay,' Josh said.

'Seriously, I think we should dry off all the balconies just in case,' Willow said. 'I'm guessing the cleaning crew came in and mopped them.'

'Polished them, more like. That floor was as slick as butter,' Tiana said.

'Right, well, we should put a towel down to make sure it's not slippery anymore. And I'm going to complain to our holiday rep.'

'I haven't seen any holiday rep,' Josh said.

'No,' Willow conceded. 'Well, I'll shoot them an email. They need to be aware of what happened.'

She glanced over at Tiana. She was putting a brave face on it, but she was still trembling slightly and Willow still felt the adrenaline coursing through her own veins.

'I think we should have a night in tonight,' she suggested. 'Watch a rom-com, overdose on popcorn.'

'Sounds good,' Tiana agreed.

'Boy's night it is!' Hugo gave Josh a friendly punch. 'We're going to hit the clubs.'

Spence wandered over and she told him what they had planned.

'You should go with them,' she said softly.

She leaned towards him. 'Seriously. I think Tiana needs to stay home and chill tonight. And I need to keep an eye on her. That was a nasty fall.'

'Okay,' he said, still sounding unhappy. 'You don't have to explain yourself to me.'

'Besides, I need you to keep an eye on the other two, make sure they don't do anything crazy.'

He nodded. 'Josh is such a lightweight we'll probably be home by nine.'

'True.'

LATER, they bought Bulgarian hotdogs from the kiosk and headed down to the beach. The sea shimmered, a bright blue-green colour that was so beautiful Tiana instantly pulled out her phone to take pictures.

They found six sun loungers together, each shaded with a straw parasol.

'I'm going for a swim,' said Lia.

'I'll come with you,' Willow said, jumping up. She followed her friend down to the water and they splashed about for a while. It was a little cool, but not too cold.

'You're burning,' Lia said.

'Dammit!' Willow's pale skin was a rag to the bright Bulgarian sun. She returned to her sun lounger and pulled out the suntan lotion.

'Here, let me do that,' Spence said. She sat in front of him while he rubbed it onto her back and shoulders.

'All your freckles are joining up.'

She waited for him to finish, but he kept rubbing the lotion in.

'I think that's enough.'

'I know, I just like touching your body. Can you blame me?'

She smiled and picked up her book. He was doing that thing again, gazing at her.

'You're so beautiful.'

'I know.' She turned the page and kept reading.

When she looked up, she saw the girl she had seen the night before, her long dark hair swishing around her as she splashed about with her friends.

Hugo was getting kitted up with a kiteboard. She took some pictures of him surfing on the water, then gliding up, hovering above the waves.

Spence watched too.

'Do you want to try it?' she asked.

He shook his head. 'Not my kind of thing.'

Josh and Lia went to get ice-creams. They seemed to be having an intense conversation. She glanced in their direction and saw their heads bent together. Their faces looked serious, and Lia's words drifted over to her.

'Never really took me seriously…I don't know if I can…'

As she watched, Josh hugged Lia and spoke in his calm, reassuring way. Whatever they were talking about was clearly private, but it confused Willow as to why Lia was having a heart to heart with her brother rather than her.

She returned to her book, determined to read at least a chapter, but she soon felt her eyes closing, and the book slipped from her grasp as she fell asleep.

She was woken by Hugo returning from his lesson, water glistening on his arms as he shed his wetsuit.

'That was amazing! Total buzz!'

She smiled. It was nice to see this side of him, not showing off for once, just living in the moment. She glanced at Spence, but he had his arms folded firmly across his chest, as if he objected to her talking to him. Well tough. She was not his personal property. She would talk to whomever she liked.

WILLOW WAS PUTTING pizza in the oven as Spence, Josh, and Hugo headed out for their night on the town. Lia and Tiana had already changed into their pyjamas and were sitting on the sofa with a large bowl of popcorn.

'What are we watching?' Willow asked as she joined them.

'It's a classic Nineties rom com,' Lia said. 'My mum loves this one.'

Willow looked over at the screen. Her own mother preferred fantasy, preferably as far removed from real life as possible. No romantic fiction for her. She sometimes wondered if things would have been different if her father were still alive.

'The lead guy isn't even hot,' Tiana complained. 'I mean, Spence, Josh and Hugo are all hotter than him.'

'All of them?' Willow spluttered.

'I wouldn't say no,' Tiana said with a smile.

'Who do you fancy the most out of the three of them?' Lia asked.

'Josh, obviously,' Tiana said.

Lia tilted her head. 'I don't know, Hugo's quite cute too. I like a man who can make me laugh.'

'Hugo's a spoilt rich kid,' Willow said.

'Ex rich kid,' Lia said. 'Didn't his folks go bankrupt?'

Willow nodded. 'I don't get how they can still afford expensive holidays. I suppose some people just know how to play the system.'

'I like his sense of humour,' Lia said. She reached for the popcorn and stuffed a handful into her mouth.

Willow couldn't deny that Hugo was funny. 'But his jokes

are never about himself, are they? They're always at someone else's expense.'

She didn't say so, but she had heard Hugo make plenty of jokes about the size of Lia's butt.

'Okay, if you had to marry one, shag one and kill one, how would that go?' Tiana said. 'I'd marry Josh, Shag Spence and kill Hugo.'

Lia giggled. 'Marry Josh, Shag Hugo and kill Spence. Sorry Willow!'

Willow raised her eyes to the ceiling. 'Marry Spence, Shag Hugo and kill Josh. Easy.'

Tiana gave her the side eye. 'I can't believe you both killed my husband.'

'Hey, you slept with mine!'

They all fell about laughing.

Willow's phone beeped. She looked down and saw a text from Josh. 'Having a great night!' There was a picture of him and Hugo, with Spence on their shoulders, waving a pint of beer in the air.

Lia and Tiana leaned into look.

'You'd think they'd put Josh on their shoulders, since he's the lightest.'

'You'd think,' Willow said, gazing at the picture. They looked like they were having a great night. She just hoped they weren't going too crazy.

Tiana pulled out her make up pack and handed out facemasks.

'What do you want, chocolate, strawberry or kiwi?'

'Are we wearing them or eating them?' Willow asked.

'They smell just like the real thing,' Tiana enthused. 'These are the latest in VivaLux's summer skincare selection.'

'I want kiwi,' Lia said.

'I'll take strawberry,' Willow said.

They ripped open the packets. There was a pungent smell, like gone off fruit. Tiana dipped a finger into hers and began smearing it all over her face. Willow tied back her hair and did the same. She didn't usually go in for facemasks. She didn't have the patience to sit about and wait for them to dry. But today was different. She was here to relax. This was going to be fun.

She applied a thin layer all over her face. Lia and Tiana used much more, scooping all the gunk from their packets and adding it to the mess on their faces. They looked hilarious.

'Facemask selfie!' Tiana said, pulling them in for a picture. 'Is it okay if I use this for my Instagram?'

'Sure,' Willow said. It wasn't like anyone would be able to recognise her.

They flopped down on the sofa and waited for the product to do its magic. Willow itched to touch hers. It felt odd, having all that gloopy mixture on her face. She could feel it hardening and her muscles tensed as it set like concrete.

'It tingles,' Lia said. 'My cheeks feel hot.'

'That's just the mask doing its job,' Tiana said.

'I don't know, I feel like it's starting to burn.' Willow jumped up and ran to the bathroom, where she splashed her face with water. She stared at herself in the mirror. Her cheeks were flushed, and she felt like she had covered her nose in chillies.

Lia burst in. 'I need to get this off!'

She moved out of the way and Lia desperately scrubbed her face.

'It's eating my flesh!' she moaned, rubbing vigorously.

'Careful, don't get it in your eyes.'

Willow walked back out to the living room. Tiana was still wearing hers.

'It won't have any effect,' she said crossly. 'You both washed it off too early.'

'I'm pretty sure ours were bad,' Willow said. Her face still felt raw.

Lia emerged from the bathroom.

'Guys, my face is swelling up!'

Willow looked at her. She was right. Her cheeks looked huge. She dashed to the fridge. 'Let's get some ice on it.'

Tiana just stood there. Willow turned and looked at her. 'I'd get that off your face right now if I were you.'

She followed Tiana to the bathroom. By the time she had got the water running, Tiana was moaning with pain.

'My skin! It feels like it's smoking. Oh my god, what's happening?'

The smoke alarm emitted a loud beep, and Willow looked at her in horror. Tiana rubbed harder and the alarm got louder. Willow jerked her head up.

'The pizza!'

She opened the bathroom door to find angry black smoke wafting in from the kitchen.

And then she saw the flames.

CHAPTER FIVE
WILLOW

Willow's eyes stung as she rushed into the kitchen. She grabbed the pot holders and threw open the oven door. She was met with billowing smoke and flames licking at the pizza on the top shelf. She must have turned on the grill instead of the oven. She switched it off, the smell of charred pepperoni filling her nostrils as she pulled out the burnt mess and dropped it onto the stone floor. Then she swatted at the flames until they went out.

Meanwhile, Lia climbed up onto a chair to dismantle the blaring smoke alarm.

'What the hell's going on?' Tiana asked, emerging from the bathroom.

Willow tried not to scream. Tiana's face was covered in welts.

'The pizza caught fire,' Lia said. Her eyes were red and puffy and her cheeks were huge.

'Have you been selling those face packs?' Willow asked Tiana.

'No, they were free samples. I guess they are still prototypes.'

'I guess that explains why I look like a guinea pig,' Lia said, looking at herself in Tiana's compact.

Willow walked around, throwing open the windows.

'We are cursed. Bloody cursed.'

They sank back down on the sofa. For a few minutes, nobody said anything. Tiana kept checking her face in the mirror. 'Definitely a bad batch,' she muttered. She pulled out her phone and started texting rapidly.

'This product launches next week. I need to warn my boss.'

'What are we going to do about dinner?' Lia asked.

Willow let out a breath. 'I'll see if I can get us a takeaway. Do you want to come?'

'Not looking like this,' Tiana said, horrified.

Willow glanced at Lia. Her cheeks were still huge. 'Get some more ice on that,' she said. She checked her own reflection. Her skin was already starting to calm down, thank goodness. She grabbed her wallet and stepped outside.

Spence and Hugo were staggering towards her, holding up Josh between them.

She rushed out onto the path to meet them.

'What the hell's wrong with him?'

'He's wasted,' Spence said.

'What, already?'

Hugo didn't look so good either. He let go of Josh and leaned into the flower beds to heave.

'It's green!' he yelled triumphantly. 'My puke's green!'

He seemed way too happy about it.

'It's not supposed to be green,' Willow said, passing him a wad of tissues. She looked at Spence.

'Get them into the house. I'll be back in ten minutes.'

She headed outside and took a couple of deep breaths. What the hell was going on? She needed to get control of this holiday again. She could just imagine how her mum would react if she were here right now. She had been dead set on proving how grown up they all were, how they didn't need parental guidance, but so far it had been one train-wreck after another.

The sea breeze cooled her cheeks as she neared the pool. She saw a couple of young people swimming in the dark. The water must have been cold, but that didn't stop them laughing and having fun. She realised they were probably locals who had snuck in for a free swim. They weren't doing any harm, she supposed. Kelly's kiosk was closed for the night, so she headed for the road that led down to the beach. She saw lights down that way, and the faint rumble of music.

She had been walking for a couple of minutes when she heard footsteps behind her. She glanced quickly over her shoulder, but she couldn't see anyone. Usually, when she went out late at night, she liked to hold her keys in her pocket. It made her feel safer. But she didn't have any keys this time. All she had was her phone and wallet. She glanced behind her again. The trees were swaying wildly, as if someone or something had just brushed past them.

The breeze rustled the dry grass at the side of the path. She swallowed hard and picked up her pace, wishing she'd asked Spence to come with her. She was almost there now. She might as well keep going.

As she stepped onto the sandy beach, her heartbeat slowed to a steady rhythm. The dark ocean waves crashed against the shore and there were a handful of people milling about. A group of men were grilling kebabs down by the water, music blaring from a speaker.

She noticed a brightly lit pier and made her way towards it, still feeling a little on edge from her creepy walk. The sign at the entrance flickered in Cyrillic, but there was a small English sign in the window that caught her attention. It read:

'Golden Hour.'

What did that mean? Was it the name of the bar, or a hint

at the services they provided? She couldn't be sure, but she headed for it anyway and pushed open the door.

The smell of stale beer and salty ocean air hit her as she stepped inside. The only other customer was a rugged man perched on a worn barstool. His scruffy T-shirt and shorts seemed to blend with the decor. She walked up to the counter, taking in the various trinkets and decorations adorning the shelves behind it - shells, sea glass, and large jars filled with coloured sand.

'Hi, do you serve food?' she asked hopefully. 'Pizza?'

'Yes, I can make you a lovely pizza,' the bar man said with a smile.

'Two please.'

'Oh, you are very hungry tonight? I cook. You wait.'

'Thank you.'

She sat at the bar and he poured her a small glass of Rakia.

'On the house. While you wait.'

'Thanks.'

She sipped it slowly.

'You're English?' the other customer said, raising his own glass.

'Yes.'

He peered at her closely. 'You are peeling like an orange.'

She nodded regretfully. She didn't feel like explaining about the facemask, and besides, she wasn't sure he would understand. She took out her phone and checked her reflection. She wished she had thought to put some cream on.

There was a new text from her mum:

'Hope you're both having a lovely time! Send me a pic!'

She laughed out loud. There was no way she was going to let her mother see her like this.

'What is funny?' the man asked.

'Nothing, just my mum checking up on me.'

She was low on charge, so she slipped her phone back into her pocket.

He nodded with approval. He did not have his phone out, she noticed. He just sat there, enjoying his drink. Nothing wrong with that, but Willow was used to doing something: watching TV or flipping through a book. To do nothing felt odd, somehow. Unnatural.

She was intensely aware of the noise he made as he swallowed a gulp of his drink. He could probably hear her too, though she only took a few careful sips. She had no idea how strong her Rakia was, and she was not about to end up like Josh and Hugo.

The bar man came back with two cardboard boxes containing her pizzas and she paid.

'Blagodarya,' she said.

As she picked up the boxes, the other customer looked up from his beer.

'You watch yourself on the way home,' he said.

She forced herself to meet his eyes. 'Why?'

Had he sensed there was someone out there? Heard something she might not like?

He looked at her over the top of his glass. 'A woman on her own can't be too careful.'

She didn't like the way he said that, as if she was doing something wrong just by being out. She forced herself to meet his gaze, and he had the grace to look down into his beer. He swallowed the dregs, leaving a foamy imprint on his moustache.

The bar man went to the door and opened it for her, and she walked out, with a final cry of:

'Blagodarya!'

'Do skora!' the man replied. She thought that meant 'goodbye.'

It was darker now, although the moon shone through the trees. She felt the same movement in the shadows, but this time she didn't look round. She walked fast, shifting the hot boxes in her arms. It was so uncomfortable carrying them like this.

She heard a flutter up in the trees and her heart beat faster. She speed walked back up the hill, not stopping until she reached the place where the path segmented with the resort. Then she set the boxes down on the ground for a moment and rested against the sign. It wobbled a little under her weight.

The swimmers were gone from the pool now. Slowly, she walked towards the edge and stared down into the shadowy waters. She slipped off one shoe and dipped her toe in, relishing the coolness of the water. There was a ripple in her reflection, and a long shadow, as if someone was standing right behind her. She turned abruptly, but there was no one. Unless they were now hidden in the shade of the palm trees. She caught her breath and shoved her foot back in her shoe. It felt wet and squelchy. She grabbed the pizza boxes and hurried towards the villa.

The lights were on and she could hear Tiana's voice, loud and laughing, as she dashed up the steps. Bursting through the door, she dumped the pizzas on the coffee table and bolted the door behind her. Tiana and Lia lazed in front of the TV, watching a film in Bulgarian with English subtitles. Lia had a bag of frozen vegetables pressed to each cheek.

'Is that swelling going down?'

'A bit.'

Lia opened the pizza boxes and they all reached for a slice. Willow was just about to take her first bite when a loud, retching sound echoed through the house. Tiana grabbed the remote and turned up the volume.

'Hugo?'

'No, that's Josh,' Lia said.

Willow rose from her seat and headed for the boy's room. Josh lay on the bed and the whole room reeked of vomit.

'You look like shit,' she told him. He couldn't even muster a smile.

'My stomach hurts so much.' There were tears in Josh's eyes and his face was deathly pale.

She placed a hand on her brother's forehead. 'You're burning up. What did you have for dinner?'

'We didn't bother with food. We just went straight to the bar.'

'Of course you did. Which one?'

'All of them. I got thrown out of the last one for projectile vomiting.'

She clapped a hand over her mouth. 'Embarrassing.'

'Not funny. I feel like I'm dying.'

He looked at her fearfully and she spotted Reggie, his teddy bear poking out from under his pillow. Normally, she would have teased him about it, but not now. He looked so ill.

Hugo emerged from the bathroom and sat shakily on his bed.

'How much did you drink?' she asked.

He shook his head in bewilderment. 'Just a few beers. We really didn't have that much.'

'Shots?'

'Only a couple.'

'What was in them?'

'I don't know.'

All at once, he shot to his feet and rushed past her to the bathroom.

Spence poked his head out of their bedroom. 'Is he okay?'

'Does it sound like he's okay?' said Hugo.

Willow ignored him. 'How are you feeling?' she asked Spence.

'Fine. I didn't drink much.'

'Did you have the shots?'

'Yeah.'

She frowned. 'Weird.'

'Not really. Josh has always been a lightweight.'

'But Hugo...'

'Like I said, I drank slowly. The other two were on a mission.'

Her screen lit up with an incoming call. Without thinking, she answered.

'Hi Mum!'

'Hi darling. Are you having a lovely time?'

'Brilliant!'

'Is Josh there? He's not answering his phone.'

She forced herself to laugh. 'He's just gone into the club, Mum. I'm going to go in too now. Speak to you tomorrow?'

'Okay, have fun!'

She hung up and looked down at Hugo, who was now writhing on the floor in agony.

'That's it. I'm taking you both to the hospital.'

CHAPTER SIX
PATSY

Three Months Earlier

Josh and Willow came crashing in from school in much the same manner as they had always done. Josh tossed his bag and coat onto a chair and headed straight for the kitchen, where he began rifling through the fridge, picking out ingredients for a triple decker sandwich. Willow, meanwhile, flopped in front of the TV. She changed the channel without asking, whilst simultaneously staring at her phone.

Patsy knew better than to ask her children how their day had been. She sat at the table, sifting through the emails for her crochet club lunch, when both Willow and Josh appeared in front of her, standing side by side like the twins in The Shining. She could see from their faces that they were conspiring. They were always hatching plots, those two. Willow had been involving Josh in elaborate schemes since he could sit up in his crib. She recalled baby Josh bum shuffling across the floor as Willow climbed onto a chair to get down the biscuit tin from the top of the cupboard. And when they became teenagers, Willow would forge them both IDs to get into clubs. Whatever they were up to, they were in it together.

She looked at them now and sensed the pent up excitement in their body language, even as they struggled to keep their faces neutral.

Willow made a loud smacking sound with her lips. Josh darted a glance at her. She wasn't the most patient of people. She wanted to come out with it, but clearly Josh was going to be the one to pitch.

'So we were thinking...' he began. He widened his stance a little, combed a hand through his hair and darted a glance at himself in the reflexion of the glass cabinet opposite, the one that displayed their family's haphazard collection of crystal animals and silver spoons.

'Yes?' Patsy waited, wondering what they wanted this time. Were they going to start on about the car again? Willow had already passed her test. Josh was still learning. They thought she should buy them a car to share. They'd found a couple of reasonably priced options, but Patsy was hesitant to help them as she worried about them getting into accidents. Young people could be careless, especially young men. She preferred that they matured a little more before they took that leap.

'As you know, we'll be finishing school this summer.'

'How could I forget?'

Willow already had a part-time job at a local furniture shop. Josh wasn't even looking. He assumed that the perfect job would just fall into his lap.

'So we were thinking, what with all the exam stress, we totally deserve a holiday.'

Patsy smiled. 'Do you think?'

She had already considered this. She had been toying with the idea of booking a short family getaway. They hadn't been abroad since before Covid and she ached for the warmth of the Mediterranean. They had had some lovely summer holidays, down in Devon and Cornwall. A week with their aunt in Wales. But she craved the near certainty of the European sun.

'Anywhere in particular?'

'Bulgaria,' Willow said.

'Bulgaria?'

'It's really beautiful there, Mum, and a lot cheaper than most of the other European countries. They get a lot of British tourists, so language shouldn't be a problem.'

'Sounds like you've already thought this through.'

'Have a look at this,' Josh said, producing his iPad. He set it down on the table and clicked on the touchpad. Instantly, the screen was filled with palm trees and beautiful pale yellow beaches. The sea was so green it was almost turquoise. She could almost taste the salt.

'Looks beautiful!'

'The prices are good Mum, look.'

She nodded. It looked better than the places they usually went to. And this was for a whole villa.

'I'll need to read up a bit.'

'Lia's mum said it was alright with her.' Willow said.

'And Hugo's.'

Patsy blinked. 'You want to bring Lia and Hugo?'

'And Tiana. If she can get the time off work. Look at these villas…' he clicked again, and she found herself looking at a row of pretty villas, overlooking a large swimming pool.

They weren't looking for a family holiday at all. This was a young person's holiday. Without parents.

'I want to go for my eighteenth,' Josh said, his hands clasped together. 'I know you said a car wasn't in your budget. But a holiday?'

He looked at her with those large, soulful eyes of his and she didn't know how to say no.

'Let me do my research,' she said. 'I need to check all this out. Make sure it's safe.'

Willow's brows knitted together. 'The others want to go ahead and book it. The prices could go up in a week.'

'Leave it with me.'

Willow's jaw tightened. She and Patsy locked eyes for a moment until Josh nudged Willow's elbow.

'Let's leave Mum to think about it,' he said softly.

Willow reluctantly broke eye contact. Her gaze shifted to the clock and then to the door.

'Fine. I'll go and do my homework.'

She gave Patsy one last look before she stomped up the stairs.

Josh threw her an apologetic smile and trailed after her, but Patsy got the message. Willow was not going to take no for an answer. If Patsy didn't help fund this holiday, they'd be going anyway, and then she would lose all control over the details.

What was she going to do? She hated the idea of them going off on their own. The fact their friends would be going too made it even worse. And then there was the problem of Spence. Willow hadn't explicitly mentioned her boyfriend, but they'd been seeing each other for months. Their over the top displays of public affection showed no signs of abating. She hoped he wouldn't be going on this holiday. Hopefully, he would be too broke to afford it. The boy was work shy and had left a perfectly good job at the department store because he didn't agree with them selling fake fur coats. She had never said as much to Willow, but she rather hoped she would tire of him and move onto someone more suitable. A nice boy like Josh's friend Hugo, perhaps. At least he had manners.

'Thanks Mum.'

With that, Josh walked out of the room, leaving Patsy to stare at the screen.

With a sigh, she rang Lia's mother, Fenella.

'They'll be alright,' Fenella said. 'They'll have each other.'

'That's what I'm worried about,' Patsy said. 'Do you think

one of us should book the villa next to theirs so we can keep an eye on them?'

Fenella laughed. She assumed Patsy was joking.

Patsy shook herself. What was she saying? She had to let them go at some point, and they were good kids, they really were. She closed her eyes and tried not to let the dark thoughts slip in. She knew she clung to her children tighter than other mothers did. That's what came of being an only parent. She knew there was no way to stop them, and yet her gut was screaming at her that she shouldn't let them go.

'LIA AND TIANA are ready to book,' Willow said two days later. 'Their parents are cool about it.'

Patsy gazed into her daughter's intelligent eyes. No one would call Willow beautiful, but she had a strong jawline, and a determination that made people pay attention. She was glad she was assertive, but it scared her at the same time. Willow was going to do what she wanted with her life, and Patsy could only watch.

In the two days since her children had announced their plan, she had read as much as she could about the resort, watched a couple of YouTube videos, and checked forums to see if there had been reports of crime in the area. By all accounts, it would be quiet the week of Josh's birthday. It seemed like the ideal time to go. She heaved a long sigh and reached into her handbag for her wallet. The deposit was only a hundred pounds. She could afford that.

'Alright,' she said.

Josh and Willow stood over her as she made the payment. It was hard to concentrate with the two of them peering over her shoulder. As soon as she had finished, they whooped and hugged her and then hugged each other.

She smiled as she watched them prance around the room in a celebratory dance. Josh was doing all his moves, hamming it up. Willow was taking it more seriously, spinning about, performing kicks and pike jumps like an American cheerleader. Patsy forced herself to clap and smile, but her stomach felt like it was filled with cement.

When the dance ended, they thundered up the stairs to call their friends. Patsy went to the fridge and pulled out a bottle of wine. She poured herself a large glass and sipped it without really tasting it. Only god knew what they would get up to in Bulgaria. Drinking and partying with no one to keep them in check. She felt like she was going to be sick.

She went back online and found Paradise Palms on a travel forum. The reviews for the resort looked good, and she felt a little less worried. She should be proud, she told herself. She had raised two strong, spirited children all by herself and they would soon be ready to spread their wings. She was about to close the tab when she noticed a new post, right at the top of the thread. She clicked on it, her eyes widening.

> Hi, I'm Kelly, 56. I run the kiosk at Paradise Palms. I serve soft drinks and ice-creams, and all kinds of food. Open from breakfast until 7pm every day. I'm originally from Lancashire, but I moved over here ten years ago. Feel free to ask me any questions!

Instantly, Patsy wrote back:

Hi Kelly! My kids are coming to Paradise Palms in August. It's their first holiday away from me, so I'm a bit nervous. They'll be coming with a group of friends.

Kelly replied:

I wouldn't worry. They'll be fine. It's a lovely resort. Very friendly.

Patsy thought for a moment. What did she want to know?

Is there a lot of crime in the area?

Kelly:

There is a bit of low-level crime, but on the whole it's safe.

She swallowed. That didn't sound very reassuring.

Are you sure? Maybe they would be better off going to France?

Kelly:

You'll find crime everywhere. It's best to go somewhere small, like Paradise Palms. But if you're really worried, I offer a teen minding service for a small fee. Keep a discrete eye on them from a distance. Check they're getting back to their villa okay at night, that sort of thing. Because I run the kiosk, they'll be talking to me, anyway. I'm like part of the furniture.

Patsy thought about it for a moment.

Can you tell me more?

Kelly:

No problem. Why don't we Facetime?

Patsy took her up on her offer of a video call.
She waited nervously for Kelly to flash up on the screen. At first, she could only hear her voice. She had a soothing northern accent, calm and gentle. Then her face popped up and Patsy saw that she did indeed look just like her profile. A little weathered, with frizzy hair in a slightly unfashionable style. She also had a large bosom that somehow made her look motherly.

For a moment, her face was frozen on the screen, then she came to life, smiling broadly.

'Ah, there you are!'

There was something so warm in that smile, so familiar. It felt almost as if she were talking to an old friend.

'Let me tell you a bit more about the resort. The stuff they don't tell you in the guidebooks. The first thing you've got to know is it's small. Nothing like the neighbouring resorts along Sunny Beach. We get our share of tourists, but they come in waves. Some weeks it's quiet as anything, other weeks it's busier. There's enough for them to do, with the beach and the bars and whatnot. But it's not so big anyone's going to get lost. It's calmer. Nicer, in my humble opinion.'

'And what about the service you provide?'

Kelly's smile broadened. 'You can think of me as a babysitter. I won't enforce their bedtimes, or tell them off if they eat junk for dinner, but I'll be there keeping an eye on them. Having a gentle word with them if I feel they need a little help. It won't look odd. They'll just see me as a member of staff.'

'Is there a lot of staff?'

'We have club reps, but they aren't here all the time. They get sent to the bigger resorts.'

'So what do I do to get this started?'

'You can send me £25 through PayPal. You don't have to do that now. A week before the holiday is soon enough. Don't forget to send me some pictures of them too, so I know who to look out for. And any additional needs. I had a young woman with diabetes out here last week. Her mum and dad just wanted me to keep an extra eye, but she was absolutely fine.'

'Glad to hear it. There's nothing like that. Mine are healthy and fairly sensible most of the time. I can't speak for some of their friends.'

'Send their pictures too, if you've got them. Best to be prepared!'

The Beach

'Thank you. You've really put my mind at rest.'

'And don't worry, I'm not going to intrude on the kids' holiday in any way. I'll just make sure they're having fun in a healthy way and if there's an emergency of some sort, I'll ring you straight away. I can also keep you updated throughout the week, let you know how they are getting on.'

'That would be great!'

She felt a little guilty as she ended the call, but it was wonderful to have some peace of mind.

CHAPTER SEVEN
WILLOW

Now

Josh was shivering uncontrollably.

'I think he's hallucinating,' Spence said.

His eyes looked glassy and threaded with red veins from all that vomiting. His skin was ashen and slick with sweat. She could sense the fear radiating off him as he pointed a trembling finger at them.

'I'm going to die! We're all going to die.'

Spence sat calmly beside him, long legs crossed, hands folded in his lap. 'Calm down, mate. You're going to be just fine.'

Josh shook his head. 'Can't you see it? Evil is everywhere. It followed us home from the bar.'

Willow bit her lip. 'What the hell did you drink?'

Outside, the taxi honked its horn.

'Go and talk to the driver,' she told Spence. 'Keep him occupied while I get these two into the cab. Don't draw attention to the fact they're sick.'

She struggled to keep Josh upright as they stumbled towards the car, his body weak and unsteady. Hugo seemed to

The Beach

be fairing better, but the stench of vomit clung to both of them.

Spence dutifully sat in the front passenger seat and quizzed the driver about the local area.

'Not many tourists this week?'

'No.'

'Does it ever get busy?'

'Yes, of course.'

'Must be nice living near the sea?'

'I love the sea,' Willow piped up from the back. Josh was falling asleep on her, his head resting in her lap, while Hugo moaned at every bump in the road.

The driver's face contorted with anger, his nostrils flaring as he spoke. 'Living by the sea, it's not all sunshine and rainbows. Everybody loves it, but they don't treat it with respect. Tourists come with their inflatables and act like it's a giant paddling pool. Well, I can tell you, it's not. The sea is treacherous, more powerful than you can ever imagine. It will swallow you whole and leave nothing but bones. You won't even have time to scream for help.'

They all fell silent, and no one dared breathe another word until they lurched to a stop outside the hospital.

'I ought to charge you double,' the driver said. 'My cab stinks like I've been transporting rotting fish.'

'Sorry,' Willow gave him a generous tip, hoping to make amends. He pocketed it, but his face remained sour.

'You can walk back,' he said, as they stumbled out. 'I don't want your rotten fish germs in my cab.'

'Thank you. It was nice to meet you too,' Willow yelled after him.

Josh leaned heavily on her as she guided him through the hospital doors. His hands were like ice blocks and he walked like it was his first time on roller blades. They approached the front desk and spoke with a frazzled receptionist, who spoke

English with such a strong accent that she had to repeat everything three times.

She handed Willow a stack of forms and Josh stood there shivering violently while she filled them in, then they headed into the crowded waiting room. It was a grubby-looking room, filled with uncomfortable chairs and magazines, all in Bulgarian. After a while, a young nurse came to check on them.

'Alcohol is a poison,' he said sternly. 'And the drinks are strong here. You are not meant to drink them all in one night.'

He took their vitals and advised them to sit quietly and drink plenty of water.

'I still don't get how you got so drunk,' Willow said after the nurse left. 'Seriously, you weren't even gone that long.'

'Long enough for you to try to burn the house down,' Hugo shot back.

'I'm not used to that oven,' Willow said. 'But seriously, do you think there might have been something wrong with the drink? Could someone have drugged you?'

'I hardly think so,' Hugo said, folding his arms.

'Maybe they planned to rob you or something?'

Josh leaned his head on her shoulder, his eyes half closed. 'Am I dead yet?'

'Drink some more water,' Willow said. 'You'll feel better soon.'

In response, Josh got up and ran to the toilet.

He returned ten minutes later, clutching his stomach. 'I feel like I've been turned inside out.'

A doctor emerged from a set of double doors and approached them.

'Hello, I'm Doctor Labackova. I hear you can't handle your drink?'

Hugo went beetroot red, but Josh was beyond the point of caring. She winked at them.

'Just trying to lighten the mood. Now, let me check how you are doing.'

The florescent lights hummed above them as she checked some details on her clipboard.

'You both need some fluids. So I think it's best to admit you for the night.'

'Are we covered for this?' Josh asked in an undertone.

'Don't worry about all that,' Willow said. 'That's what all those forms were about.'

The doctor looked at Willow. 'Well, I have good news for you. There is yet more paperwork. If you go to the front desk, they will sort you out.'

Willow grimaced. 'Thanks.'

'To be honest, it's not the first time we've seen tourists with these symptoms,' the doctor said. 'You need to be careful what you drink. Stick to familiar brands.'

She nodded. She already knew all this. It was her idiot brother who needed to hear it.

Josh and Hugo were shown to their room while she worked through more forms.

'I didn't write this much for my coursework,' she complained.

'You're doing a great job,' Spence said, watching her.

'I've had better date nights.' She mustered up a smile. 'What a bloody nightmare! First Tiana, then this.'

'We've still got five more day's holiday. It can only be up hill from here.'

'Now you've jinxed it.'

She handed in all the paperwork, and they headed outside. It was too late to get a bus, and she didn't want to deal with the taxi company again, so they began the long walk home. It was dark but beautiful. Spence's hand felt a little tight in hers, but she felt safe with him beside her.

'You know what? You're going to make an awesome mum one day.'

She concentrated on the pavement. 'I'm not sure I want kids, if this is what it's like.'

'Don't say that.'

'I'm serious. I'm beginning to get a new found respect for my mum.'

'You will want kids, when the time's right. I know you.'

She shook her head. There was no point arguing about it. She just wanted to get back to the villa so she could sleep.

Josh and Hugo were released from the hospital the following afternoon. To celebrate their return, they all went out for dinner. Josh abstained from the booze, but Willow was annoyed when Hugo ordered a beer.

'For god's sake, you've just had alcohol poisoning,' she said.

'Sorry, Mum.'

She shook her head. 'Some people really don't know what's good for them.'

The food came. Willow tucked into a delicious Shopska salad with stuffed peppers. Spence poked his food with a fork. He had ordered sausages, but they had come with a complimentary salad. The Bulgarians sure did love their salads! The problem was that Spence didn't do vegetables.

When they finished eating, the waiter came over with a dish that looked like a sweet flaky pastry.

'Oh, we didn't order dessert,' Willow said.

He smiled. 'I know but I wanted to give you something as sweet as you are,' he winked at her, and backed away, leaving her to look at the pretty dish of baklava. She stuck a fork in.

'Delicious!' she proclaimed with a smile. She turned to Spence. 'Try some.'

He shook his head tightly.

'What's wrong?'

'What's wrong?' he exploded. 'That waiter was clearly coming on to you.'

Willow placed a hand on his shoulder. 'He was just being nice. They probably had this left over.'

'He wants to get into your pants.'

'I wouldn't say no,' Tiana said, reaching across and grabbing a piece of baklava. 'He was pretty hot.'

'There you go. Tiana can have him.'

Spence didn't smile. Willow paid their share of the bill and pulled him out the door.

'I'm so full. Let's walk it off a bit.'

'Okay.'

Hand in hand, they followed the now familiar path down to the shore. The sun was setting, casting a warm glow over the horizon. They stopped and listened to the rhythmic sound of waves crashing against the beach. Spence pointed towards the sky, his finger tracing the line where it met the sea. His eyes gleamed as he took in the vast expanse of water.

'I could picture us living somewhere like this one day.'

When Willow didn't answer, he stooped down and picked up a smooth pebble, his arm swinging back before launching it into the sea. They watched as it hit the surface with a plop, causing ripples to spread out like veins pulsing with life.

They walked back past the Golden Hour, and Willow was amused to see the man she'd met the night before, still propping up the bar. He gave her a little wave and she waved back.

'Who the hell was that?'

'Oh, I met him last night, when I went to get the pizza.'

Spence steamed ahead, up the road towards the villa and once again, Willow was left alone in the dark. It ought to have been easier since she knew the way now, but she still felt creeped out. She was angry at Spence for being so ridiculous. He hadn't always been like this. When they first got together, he had been more chilled. It was only in recent weeks he had started flipping out every time another man looked at her. And the more he did it, the more she felt herself pulling away from him. They were eighteen, for pity's sake. Did everything have to be so damned serious?

Kelly from the kiosk appeared on the path in front of her. She was hurrying along, and Willow wondered if something was wrong.

'What are you doing? You shouldn't be walking alone like this at night. It isn't safe.'

Willow's jaw dropped. 'You're out on your own too!'

'I'm not a pretty young woman, and besides, I know this area like the back of my hand. Believe me. No one can touch me.'

Willow frowned. She didn't like the way Kelly was looking at her, like she was a naughty school girl. The older woman fell into step with her, and they walked together, neither of them saying anything, all the way back to the villa.

CHAPTER EIGHT
WILLOW

Tuesday

Spence did not apologise for the way he had stormed off. He lay motionless beside her as she tried to get to sleep, and in the morning he acted as though nothing had happened, but the tension was still there and Willow felt as though there was a knot forming around her throat, making it difficult to swallow.

Hugo was feeling well enough to go kite surfing again, so they made their way down to the beach. Josh chose a sun lounger next to Willow's and Spence took the one on her other side whilst barely uttering a word. She ignored his performative sulking. He pretended he wasn't doing anything, but she noticed how his eyes didn't quite focus when he looked at her, and he pressed his lips together so they became a thin line. His gaze met hers briefly before flicking away. She picked up her book and tried to enjoy herself as best she could. She looked up and saw Tiana and Lia dancing about in the waves.

'Are you coming in?' Tiana yelled.

Smiling, she set down her book and ran down to join them. It was a little windy today, and the breeze blew sand into her eyes. She rubbed it away and saw Josh heading down to the water's edge. He looked at her with interest.

'Everything alright between you and lover boy?'

Willow glanced back at Spence. 'I don't know why he even came on this holiday, if he's determined not to enjoy himself,' she said.

'Why is he like that?'

'I have no idea.'

The girl with the long hair drifted by and they both watched her for a moment, then Willow headed into the water where Tiana and Lia were splashing about on an inflatable unicorn.

She braved the cool water and made it over to them, just as they both fell off, laughing like crazy. The unicorn got picked up by the tide and started to drift away, but Willow swam after it, using strong, fast strokes until she managed to grab hold of it and tow it back to her friends.

'Thanks!' Tiana said. 'Twenty quid, that cost me. Would be a bit of a downer if it got away.'

'Naughty Penny!' Lia said.

'Penny?'

'That's what we're calling it. Penny Wise the Uniclown.'

'Right.'

She looked over at Hugh, who had begun his kiteboarding session. She watched as he surfed a little. His body looked taut and strong as he rode the waves. One of his fellow kiteboarders fell off, but he was a natural.

'Look at Hugo!'

They watched as he rose into the air. He floated there for a short time, rising higher and higher.

It was weird to see their arrogant friend being so graceful and free. It was like watching an eagle gliding through the sky.

There was a strong breeze and his kite started to wobble erratically.

'Something's wrong!'

Willow stopped paddling. Other people were watching too. The girl with the mermaid hair was standing very still, a frown drawn across her face. She shouted a warning to the lifeguard.

Someone was yelling at Hugo, shouting instructions, but she doubted he could hear. He was swooping up and up and then whirling upside down with the wind. Her breath grew ragged as he soared high above her head, then came in fast, flying above all the people on the beach.

'Where the hell is he going?'

He was spinning like crazy. The instructor shouted again, but it was too late. His board flipped and he crashed into the side of a hotel, falling to earth like a bird that had been shot out of the sky.

CHAPTER NINE
WILLOW

The sand burned her feet as she sprinted towards Hugo. He lay on the ground, writhing in agony. A lifeguard was already attending to him, kneeling at his side. She could see that he was in pain, so she pushed through the crowd.

'Hugo!'

She gave him her hand. He clutched it tight.

'My leg!'

He screwed up his eyes in pain. She had never seen big, brash Hugo cry before.

The blaring sound of sirens filled the air as an ambulance pulled onto the beach. People parted to make way as two paramedics rushed towards them. They assessed Hugo's injuries before lifting him onto a stretcher.

'Willow…' he croaked.

'Can I come with him?' she asked.

One of the paramedics nodded. 'Yes, no problem.'

'Great, I'll just be a sec.'

She bolted back to her sun lounger and grabbed her sandals, purse, and sarong. As she turned to dash off again,

Spence caught her arm with a desperate grip. She tried to shake him off, but he held on tight.

'Hold on!'

'I have to go. I'm going with Hugo to the hospital.'

Fear flashed through his eyes.

'Don't go.'

'I have to. Hugo's hurt. He needs me.'

'I can't lose you.' His voice cracked with emotion.

Tears welled in her eyes and she bit her lip. 'You're the one pushing me away, with all your sulking and jealousy.'

She broke free from his grasp and sprinted across the hot sand, jumping in the back of the ambulance before the paramedics shut the doors.

They rocked and bumped all the way to the hospital. Willow talked non stop, trying to distract Hugo while they injected him with painkillers. By the time they arrived, his white cheeks became pink, and a dreamy look appeared in his eyes. As they pulled up outside the hospital, Willow's shoulders sagged with fatigue. She had already spent more time here than at the beach.

The paramedics lifted Hugo onto a cold metal trolley and rushed him through the automatic doors of the emergency room. She followed close behind, the rubber soles of her flip-flops squeaking against the sterile tile floor. Inside, they were directed to the cramped waiting area, and Willow positioned herself on one of the uncomfortable plastic chairs. The smell of disinfectant lingered in the air as her fingers played with the hem of her sarong. Hugo, who had been dozing for the last few minutes, woke up and looked at her. Their eyes met, and in that moment, a silent understanding passed between them.

'Thank you so much for taking care of me.'

'It's nothing.'

'And don't worry, I'm not going to start crying again.'

She smiled. 'Me either.'

He took her hand, eyes wide. 'But seriously, you are the best. I hope Spence knows how lucky he is.'

She dropped her gaze. 'He does. I know he does.'

'Look at us! This is the worst holiday ever,' he said with a laugh.

'Don't say that,' she said. 'I'm sorry you had an accident, but this is a beautiful place. It's not its fault.'

'What is it, then? I feel like someone's out to get us.'

She thought of the footsteps she had heard behind her when she had walked back from the beach bar. The sense of being followed.

'No,' she said. 'It's just bad luck, that's all. Why would anyone be after us? They don't even know us.'

'But the kite…'

'What about it?'

'It was so strange. I was doing fine. I had good control. Then all of a sudden it felt like something snapped. A string or something. Then I was flying with the wind, totally out of control. I could see the building looming towards me, but I had no way of stopping myself, so I just braced as best I could and oof!'

She shuddered, recalling the moment of impact.

'It looked terrifying,' she said. 'I think you're very brave.'

'But was it an accident?'

She fought back a wave of irritation.

'It's a dangerous sport, even if you've done it before. I saw the waiver you signed. It specifically states that on there.'

'Still. I never expected this.'

'Do you want to call your folks?'

'No, they're away on safari.'

She didn't know if he meant they were literally on safari or just on holiday. Two years at her secondary school had knocked most of the poshness out of him, but it was still there. He still said stuff like 'chaps' and 'tuck' and used way too many abbreviations. The others had teased him mercilessly for it, but Hugo had the hide of a rhino.

A nurse came in to wheel him down to X-ray.

She rose from her chair. 'I'll go and get us some coffees, shall I?'

'And a sandwich, if you can? I haven't eaten since breakfast.'

She smiled, glad he was back to himself, and headed to the little canteen.

While she was in the queue, her phone pinged.

Spence.

She slipped her phone back into her pocket without even reading his message. She couldn't deal with him right now. She piled a tray with food, including a bowl of stew for herself, then sat at a table and ate. One thing was for sure: the Bulgarian hospital food was way better than anything she'd ever had at home in England.

She returned to the waiting room, and amused herself reading an old comic book she found lying about. Some time later, she looked up to see Hugo, hopping along on crutches, his right leg in plaster.

'It's broken then?' she said. 'Do you want to see if you can get a flight home early?'

'What, and waste our magnificent villa? No, I think I'd be better off resting on the beach. Can't think of a better place to recuperate.'

'You can't get it wet, though, can you?'

'No, I'll be careful. They're letting me go, anyway. So that's good news. I am so sick of this place!'

THE NURSE CALLED them a taxi and this time they got a lovely driver, who didn't seem the least bit worried about germs. He drove way too fast though, and poor Hugo moaned every time he took a corner.

When they got back to the villa, Spence was in their room writing, so Willow decided to leave him to it. She helped set Hugo up on the sofa, propping his leg up with pillows, then texted Tiana. The others were still down the beach. She could have joined them but she decided to stay home. She could hardly leave Hugo on his own with his leg in plaster.

She rummaged about in the kitchen and returned, balancing two glasses of red wine with steady hands. She sat in the armchair and they watched whatever came on TV. He did impressions of some of the characters. He got the voices and the mannerisms spot on. She couldn't help but laugh as he transformed into Cruella de Ville, complete with wild gesticulations and an evil cackle. 'You could make a killing as a villain,' she told him.

She stopped laughing as Spence emerged from the bedroom. He looked at Hugo's leg.

'Bad luck, mate.'

He perched on the arm of Willow's chair.

'Sorry about earlier,' he murmured in her ear. 'I don't know what came over me. I just wanted this holiday to be perfect.'

'Well, you need to nip it in the bud,' she said. 'I intend to make the most of the remaining few days.'

'I hear you. From now on, I promise to be the model boyfriend.'

She looked over at Hugo, who was starting to doze off. He looked contented despite his broken leg.

THAT EVENING, they got take away and ate at the villa. All of them gathered around the coffee table, talking and laughing. A perfect evening in many ways.

Willow looked around at her brother and friends.

She refilled their wine glasses, feeling a buzz from the drinks she had already consumed. Then she raised her glass.

'To a crazy, messed up holiday!'
Everyone erupted around the table.
'I'll drink to that,' Hugo said, and they all clinked glasses.
'No wait, I'm not finished,' she said, aware that she was slurring a little.
'You all need to stop acting like fucking lemmings.'
Tiana burst out laughing.
'No, I'm serious!' Willow looked each of them in the eye. 'No more falling off balconies or kite surfing accidents or… or…alcohol poisoning. Can we just enjoy the few days we've got left without anyone else getting into trouble?'

CHAPTER TEN
WILLOW

Wednesday

The blistering midday sun beat down on Paradise Palms, creating a hazy heat that made Willow's skin sticky and caused her clothes to cling. She wiped sweat from her brow as she walked down to the pool, where Tiana sat at the side, fanning herself with a magazine, and Josh crunched the ice cubes from his rum and coke. The heat was so intense that steam rose from the surface of the glistening water.

Despite the oppressive heat, everyone seemed to be in good spirits.

'Where's Spence?' Josh asked.

'He's inside. He just wanted to get a few lines of poetry down while he was feeling inspired.'

Hugo reached into his pocket and pulled out a couple of painkillers, tossing them back with a gulp of water.

'Want me to slip a few of these into his beer?' he offered.

Willow smiled. She knew he wasn't serious, but anyway, she had a feeling they would only make Spence more morose.

The Beach

Tiana and Lia raced up and down the pool. Josh set his drink to one side and dive bombed them, just as he did when they were little.

Willow was happy sitting by the pool, watching it all. She stayed with Hugo quite a bit. She felt responsible for him. She made sure he got plenty of fluids, not just beer like he wanted but water too, because she was concerned about how alcohol would affect the painkillers he was taking.

'What are you going to do when we get home?' she asked.

He shrugged. 'I got a place at Bristol but I deferred.'

'Why?'

'I don't know. I'm just not ready.'

She was surprised to hear this. As far as she knew, Hugo already lived relatively independently. He had a self-contained cabin at the end of his parents' garden, which he treated as a bachelor pad, and they were often away, leaving him to fend for himself. What difference would it make to go away to uni?

'I only just felt like I was fitting in at school. It took me a while to understand the rules, the people. It felt like home. And going to uni, I'll have to do it all over again. I'm not even sure I want to.'

If their friends hadn't been sitting there, witnessing their conversation, she might have hugged him. Poor little rich boy.

'What about you?' he asked.

'I've got my job,' she said, without enthusiasm.

'You haven't considered uni?'

'And accumulate thousands in debt? No thanks!'

'You know what we should do? We should just go travelling. Explore the world.'

'That's just putting off grown up life.'

'I know. That's the point.'

A woman with a strong, athletic build strutted into the pool area, carrying a bag of colourful floats. She set up her equipment and turned on some lively music, which drew the attention of a group of primarily grey-haired women wearing swim caps.

'Shall we go to the beach?' Willow said.

'No way, I'm doing aqua!' Josh said, and leapt into the pool.

The women smiled at him, delighted. The instructor led the class in various exercises and Josh participated with enthusiasm, tossing balls back and forth with some of the ladies and breaking out into dance moves every now and then.

Tiana glanced at him for a moment, then she went and sat on a stall at the kiosk and got talking to Kelly's assistant, a gormless guy who didn't speak much English. They seemed to be having quite a long, involved conversation using facial expressions and exaggerated hand movements.

By the time Willow got up to order more drinks from the bar, they were kissing. She waited impatiently and cleared her throat. The unlikely couple broke apart. Tiana looked at her and grinned. Then, to Willow's disgust, she glanced behind her to see if Josh was looking.

'Two Cokes please,' she said pointedly to the man, and she handed him some money. She rather liked the Bulgarian bank notes, most of which were colourful and featured men with big moustaches.

A little later, Kelly came over to check on Hugo.

'How are you doing?' she asked. 'I heard all about your accident. It sounded terrible!'

Hugo nodded.

'You are brave, staying on after getting injured,' Kelly went on.

'Where else would I want to go?' He waved his arm around. 'I mean, this is a literal paradise.'

'His parents are away, anyway,' Willow added. 'There's no point in him going home.'

'Oh, poor love.'

The Beach

Kelly smiled at him sadly, and for a moment, Willow thought she was going to throw her arms around him, but then she seemed to think better of it.

'You must make sure you keep your whole leg under the parasol,' she said, adjusting it. 'You really don't want to get sunburned.'

'You are good to me. It's like having my mum here,' Hugo joked.

Kelly gave a little half smile, and disappeared back into the kiosk. Willow wondered if he had offended her somehow.

She rubbed her forehead. She was getting too hot. She was going to have to get in the pool in a minute.

'How long do you reckon she's been here?' Hugo asked, lowering his voice.

'Kelly? Who knows? She hasn't lost her accent though, has she?'

They both watched as Kelly cleaned the counter, then rinsed the cloth she had used and started again. It seemed to be a circular process. She finished one task and began the other. The bloke working with her sat on a stool and flipped through a magazine.

Kelly watched the pool as she worked. Her eyes scanning back and forth, as if checking all was okay. Perhaps she was feeling paranoid after Tiana's fall the other day.

The aqua class finished and the ladies all left. Josh blew them kisses, pretending to be heart broken.

Lia went back to the villa, only to emerge twenty minutes later, all done up in heavy eye make up and a short black dress Willow had never seen her in.

'Where are you off to?'

'Just going to the bar.'

Willow peered at her closely. 'What, are you meeting someone?'

Lia gave a little shrug. 'Wouldn't you like to know?'

They watched as she sauntered off.

'Do you know who she's meeting?' she asked Tiana.

'No idea.'

Josh whistled. 'It's always the quiet ones!'

THE BRIGHT BLUE sky clouded over, and Willow felt a shiver down her spine. A heavy grey cloud sailed across the sky and she grabbed her book and the suntan lotion, stuffing them back into her bag. When the downpour started, everyone scrambled out of the pool, running for their villas.

'Josh!' she yelled, holding her bag over her head to keep dry. 'Tiana! Wait!'

White lightning ripped through the sky. Seconds passed and there was a giant crash. Like a drum set being hurled from above. It was so awe-inspiring that for a moment, everybody froze and looked up at the heavens. There was a smell, like burnt wire, and then everyone seemed to come unstuck. She turned to Hugo and picked up his bag while he got himself to his feet. Josh walked back to them, and between the two of them, they helped Hugo back to the villa.

The weight of Hugo's arm around her shoulder felt good. There was a solidness to him that she was coming to like. It went with his character. Solid and dependable. He said it like it was.

They helped him onto the sofa and settled there, listening to the rain pattering on the roof.

She spotted a map on the bookshelf, in between a dogeared copy of the bible and a treasure trove of Sherlock Holmes stories.

She laid the map out on the table. She liked looking at all the streets and landmarks.

'I really want to visit Sozapol,' she said. 'The bus takes forty minutes. That would give us time to walk around the centre and check out a nice restaurant for lunch.'

The Beach

Tiana was nodding. Spence leaned back against his chair and said nothing. Was she supposed to guess what he was thinking?

'I'm happy here,' Josh said.

'I thought you wanted to see a bit of Bulgaria? You were on about the caves at the airport and we've come all this way.'

'The caves are too far, and I didn't know it was going to be so hot.'

'Why don't you girls go?' Hugo suggested. 'I would be well up for it if it weren't for this leg.'

'Alright,' Willow agreed. 'Just don't get yourselves into any trouble, alright?'

'What do you think we are, two-year-olds?' Josh said.

She met her brother's eye. 'Sometimes.'

She tried to fold the map up again, but it resisted. She fought with it, weighing it down on one end, but it sprang back up in the middle. She folded it from the other side and found herself looking at a concertina of pages. Hugo was smirking at her under his blanket.

Spence got up and headed into their room. She abandoned the map, leaving it to spring up on the table like a tent. She found Spence on the balcony, looking down at the pool with great concentration, as if trying to see something deep in the water.

She went over to him and he wrapped his arms around her, so tight she could barely breathe. She felt intense fear radiating out of him. She looked down and tried to see what he was looking at, but there was nothing but the rain dripping into the empty pool.

'What's up?'

'I don't know. I'm just…getting a feeling.'

'What sort of feeling?'

'It's hard to describe.' He turned to look at her. 'I just feel sort of unsettled, like I'm waiting for something to happen.'

'What?'

'I won't know until it happens.'

'Alright then!' She forced out a laugh. But he was giving her the chills. Because Spence was deeply attuned to his environment. And if he felt uneasy, then that meant that she probably should too.

CHAPTER ELEVEN
PATSY

Wednesday

Patsy leaned forward and pressed the Facetime icon on her phone. Kelly had said midday, but it was a few minutes past now and she still hadn't started the call. She glanced at the clock. What time would it be in Bulgaria? Were they one hour ahead or two? She couldn't remember.

Then her phone lit up, and a moment later, Kelly's face popped up on her screen. She could see in the background that it was sunny. The light reflected off the tables. People were wearing sunglasses and swimwear.

Kelly waved enthusiastically. She was always enthusiastic. Patsy could see the ice creams on display at her kiosk.

Kelly panned the camera around the pool area and she caught sight of Josh splashing about. She smiled as she looked at her boy. He looked like he was having fun.

'Have you seen Willow?' she asked.

The camera moved and there was Willow applying suntan lotion.

'They're getting on okay, then?'

'They're absolutely fine. To be honest, it's been pretty quiet here. Not many tourists.'

Patsy smiled. She was glad to hear that. She wanted her children to have fun, but she didn't want them to mix with the wrong sort.

'The weather's been amazing as well, although we are expecting a downpour later.'

Patsy already knew this. She had been tracking the resort on her weather app.

'Seriously, you can relax!' Kelly said. 'Your kids are having a great time.' She leaned in a little closer. 'Actually, I've heard one of the local girls has a thing for Josh. Not that he's noticed.'

Patsy laughed. 'They've always got a thing for Josh. It's been like that since he was a baby.'

Kelly smiled. 'He is a very handsome boy.'

She turned the camera round again, zooming in closer, so that Patsy could see right up close to Josh and Tiana. She held the camera there so long that in the end, Patsy had to finish the call.

'Thank you for the update, Kelly. I'd better get back to work.'

'Okay, and seriously, don't worry about your kids. They're having a great time, and if anything comes up, I'm always here, always watching.'

Kelly panned the camera around a final time, giving Patsy one last view of the resort. She had been about to end the call when she spotted someone talking to Lia, just outside the villa.

'Wait, is that Spence?'

She strained her eyes. Yes, it was! Willow had distinctly said he wouldn't be coming on the holiday, but here he was! Anger boiled in her chest. What else had she lied about?

CHAPTER TWELVE
WILLOW

Thursday

Willow zipped up her bag and slung it over her shoulder. 'Sure you don't want to come?' she asked Spence, who was propped up on the bed with his notebook.

'No, you go and have fun with the girls. Besides, I think someone needs to stay here and keep an eye on Hugo.'

'Josh is staying.'

'I mean, a grown up.'

She nodded and reached for her sun hat. As she turned to leave, Spence grabbed her by the waist and pulled her in for a deep, passionate kiss. His hot breath tickled her neck, and she felt his days-old stubble brushing against her cheek. A wave of desire rushed through her as she kissed him back, their bodies pressed together tightly. It might have led to something more had Tiana not knocked on the door at that moment.

'Time to leave, if we're going to get the next bus.'

Willow broke away. 'I'd better go,' she said apologetically to Spence. 'Maybe we can pick this up later?'

They walked down to the bus stop, stopping to buy bottles

of water from Kelly at the kiosk. The bus was packed. It seemed they weren't the only ones who wanted a day out. They found three seats at the back and spread out.

'I feel like we're on a school trip,' Tiana giggled.

'I wish we had seatbelts,' Willow said, as the bus swerved round a corner.

'Yes, Mum,' Tiana said.

Willow ignored her and shoved open the window to let in some air. The sun beat down with relentless intensity. The deep blue sea stretched out before her, its waves crashing against the jagged rocks below. The salty mist clung to her hair and skin as she gazed in awe at the shimmering sapphire water.

'So, who were you meeting yesterday?' Tiana asked Lia, about as subtle as a brick.

Lia shifted uneasily. 'No one. I just wanted to go out on my own for a change.'

Willow and Tiana exchanged a glance. This was weird, even by Lia's standards.

The bus dropped them off in the centre of Sozopol, and everyone surged towards the row of tourist shops. Willow tugged Tiana's arm, steering her and Lia away from the bustling crowd.

The ancient city was a timeless wonder, its streets weaving through centuries of history. They passed statues, fountains, and buildings that stood as testament to the city's rich past. They kept walking, passing a row of more modern houses in a rainbow of pastel colours. As they turned a corner, the street opened up into a bustling square, alive with the sounds of traditional music, and vendors selling handmade trinkets.

Tiana's eyes lit up at the sight. They browsed the stalls, admiring handmade crafts and fabrics.

'Hey look, they have tartan phone covers. You should get one. That's totally your brand.'

Willow smiled. 'They sell those in England.'

The Beach

Her gaze shifted to the next stall, which contained a curious collection of knick-knacks. Her fingers reached for a porcelain figurine of a woman, clutching two small children. The woman's grip looked tight and desperate, almost suffocating the children, who wore frozen smiles on their faces.

'How much?'

'10 Lev.'

'I'll take it.' She pointed to a couple of postcards. 'These too.'

'Is that for Spence?' Tiana quipped as they waited for the gift to be wrapped.

'Actually, it's for my mum. I don't normally bother but I think she'd appreciate some mail.'

'Aw. That's sweet. I'm getting mine some duty-free cigarettes at the airport.'

They left the square and continued to explore, stopping to look at a small chapel, its stone walls weathered with time.

'It could do with a repaint,' Tiana said. 'I mean, these walls would be so much more *now* in lime green, don't you think?'

Lia frowned. 'I really don't think that's the aesthetic they're going for. If anything, it should be more grey, more goth. I'd add a raven or two. Maybe a permanent thunder cloud.'

'I don't know about you two, but I'm about ready for lunch,' Willow said.

The others agreed and Lia even picked up pace at the prospect.

They found a charming little restaurant nestled on a rocky cliff overlooking the sparkling turquoise water. The scent of smoky grilled aubergine wafted through the air, enticing them to take a seat at one of the outdoor tables.

They ordered moussaka and stuffed peppers, finishing with a decadent Garash cake. They ate until they were uncomfortably full and then headed down to the beach.

'Are you and Spence okay?' Lia asked as she applied more sun cream. 'He was looking a bit less frosty this morning.'

'Yeah, we're fine. He can be a moody bugger.'

'But you love him anyway?'

'I suppose I do.'

'Do you think you'll marry him one day?'

'Jesus, we're eighteen. Who knows?'

Lia nodded her head slowly, as this confirmed whatever it was she had been thinking. She sat staring at the waves.

'You okay?' Willow asked.

'Just trying to make a decision.'

'Anything I can help with?'

Lia sighed. 'No, not really.'

'Anyone need the loo?' Tiana asked.

They both shook their heads. Willow waited until Tiana walked off, then looked at Lia.

'Are you ready to fess up about your date?'

'There was no date. I meant what I said. I just wanted a chance to socialise without you and Tiana being there.'

Willow felt her stomach drop. 'Why?'

'Because you always colour people's perceptions of me.'

'What the hell are you talking about?'

'When I'm with you, I'm always the shy one. The fat one. The quiet one. I'm sick of it. I don't want to be your side kick. I want to be the main character in my own life.'

'I don't see it that way at all. You are a main character, same as me and Tiana.'

Lia's face had gone red. 'No, you're both so loud and out there that no one even notices me. People actually refer to me as "Willow's friend" or "Tiana's friend," as if those are my names. Sometimes boys come up to me when we go out, but they don't really see me. They ask me to introduce them to you or Tiana. They want me to put in a word and I'm so sick of it. For a long time, I thought the problem was me. I thought

The Beach

I needed to reinvent myself, but after coming away on this holiday, I've realised I just need better friends.'

Willow shook her head. 'But we're your friends. We care about you.'

Lia turned her head away. 'You've got a funny way of showing it.'

Tiana returned and Lia said nothing more. They both sat and listened as Tiana recounted an amusing anecdote about wandering into the gents by mistake.

Willow tried to relax, but what Lia had said disturbed her. Was she really such a bad friend? She'd known Lia so long she took their friendship for granted. But she'd assumed Lia did too. How had she got it so wrong? She could feel the heat on her shoulders, despite the generous amounts of sun tan lotion she'd applied.

'It'll be time to catch the bus in a little while,' she said. 'Do you mind if we start packing up?'

The others agreed. Lia seemed to have perked up a bit as they walked back to the bus stop. Willow thought about telling Tiana what she had said, but decided against it. Tiana was as blunt as a bulldozer, and this situation required a little more sensitivity. Lia had always had a tendency to catastrophise and wallow. But if there was any truth in what she was saying, then Willow was going to put it right. She promised herself that she was going to make sure Lia had the holiday of a lifetime. No way would she want to ditch her and Tiana after that.

Without even knowing about her mission, Tiana played some music on her phone and started improvising some outlandish dance steps. Her enthusiasm was contagious, and soon they were all dancing about, giggling and being silly.

'Play that one again,' she told Tiana as the song came to an end.

She danced with renewed vigour. Out of the corner of her eye, she saw Lia smiling, having a good time. Willow felt her shoulders relax. Maybe Lia was just on her period. She couldn't possibly have meant what she had said. They were best friends. Always had been.

All at once, a car came careering around the corner, totally out of nowhere.

'Watch out!' she yelped, leaping out of the way.

Tiana moved fast, but Lia was too slow.

Willow felt the crunch, as if it were her own flesh. She saw Lia stagger forward, her body slamming the pavement, and her flip-flop flew up in the air, landing on the ground in front of them.

CHAPTER THIRTEEN
WILLOW

The impact forced the air from Lia's lungs. She lay on the ground, not speaking, her eyes large as saucers. Willow turned, her heart pounding in her chest as she looked in the direction of the speeding car, but all that remained was a cloud of dust hovering in its wake.

'Lia? Say something? Are you okay?' Tiana was bending over their friend.

Lia looked down at her legs. They were shaking badly, as if attached to a pneumatic drill.

'I…I think so. What…what was that?'

Willow looked at the rubbish bin that now lay on its side, with litter scattered all over the street.

'It felt like that car was coming right for us. If it wasn't for the bin, I think it would have really done some damage.'

Lia slipped her shoe back on, then looked at her phone. Her face crumpled and Willow saw that a spider web of cracks now covered the screen.

'Better your phone than you,' Willow said quietly. She replayed it again in her mind. It was weird the way that car had come out of nowhere. Almost as if it was aiming for them. She shook herself. She was being paranoid.

Tiana cleared her throat.

'I saw a cocktail bar on our way here. We should have time to get one before the bus.'

'Sod the bus,' Willow said. 'We can always get the next one.'

She kept a close eye on Lia as they sipped their cocktails. She seemed okay, but it was hard to tell with Lia. She was so guarded. It was impossible to know what she was really thinking, and she so easily could have been badly injured. It didn't bear thinking about.

While Tiana and Lia chilled, she felt stone cold sober. As they waited for the bus back to the resort, she had a feeling of heaviness in her bones. The rest of the tourists appeared to have had a great time. One older woman turned to her and spoke enthusiastically about the restaurant she had visited.

'The food was amazing! Such a selection! They even had parrot fish. Did you ever taste such fresh fish?'

Willow shook her head and forced a smile.

The woman's companion started a long monologue about the sights they'd visited. How ancient they were, how beautifully preserved. Willow tried to show her appreciation for their attempts to include her and her friends in their conversation, but her mind was elsewhere.

She found her eyes darting every so often towards the road, keeping an eye on the cars that were rounding the bend. Most of them drove safely through the town, but every once in a while there was another fast one that made her shrink back, away from the curb. She looked with concern at the large group that had congregated, all waiting for the bus. If the car that had hit Lia had come along just an hour later, there would have been a tragedy for sure. But she had a feeling mass casualties had not been the intention. Her group was the target. Just them.

The Beach

Was it possible someone had followed them to Sozopol? It would have to be a local, or else they'd have to hire a car. It sounded extreme, even in her head, but she couldn't drop the feeling that this was one accident too many.

The bus came into view. It trundled up the road, like a cow crossing the pasture, and fizzed to a stop. Her fellow passengers were in high spirits as they crammed aboard. Willow was grateful for the air conditioning as they snuggled together on the back seat. Tiana and Lia soon fell asleep, but Willow just sat there listening as the other holiday makers burst into song. Everyone was in such a happy holiday mood, but she was deep in thought, plagued by all the accidents and mishaps that had struck them so far. And suddenly, she wanted, more than anything, to speak to her mum.

As soon as the bus arrived back at Paradise Palms, she headed back to her room. She was glad to find that the boys were out, presumably at the beach, since she hadn't seen them down by the pool. She took out her phone and FaceTimed her mum.

Patsy was out in the garden when she answered. She was wearing the hideous cork hat she wore to protect herself from the sun, along with a pair of orange trousers that had last been fashionable in the 1970s. Willow smiled fondly. Her mum never wore embarrassing clothes when she went out, but in the sanctuary of her own home, all bets were off.

'It's a lovely day,' Patsy said. 'The sunshine is up at full volume. Just look at the sunflowers!'

Willow smiled indulgently. 'It's really hot here, too.'

'Have you been in the pool?'

'Not today. We went on a day out to Sozopol.'

'Lovely.'

Willow was struck by how calm her mum seemed. She didn't badger her for information the way she sometimes did. Maybe she was chilling in her old age. It was a good thing. But today, she wished she would ask more probing questions. She would love for her to ask what was wrong. It would give Willow the outlet she needed to pour out all her worries. As it was, she talked about the family dinner she had arranged to celebrate Josh's birthday. She was planning to cook all Josh's favourite foods and put on a slide show of all their favourite family memories.

'It sounds lovely,' Willow said. 'Can't wait.'

She couldn't recall her mother going to that much trouble for her eighteenth. Of course, Granny Marks had been very ill at the time, so she had been distracted. But it nagged a little, the sense that Josh was her golden child, her baby, and probably always would be.

'What about Spence?'

'What about him?'

'Will he be coming to the family dinner?'

'Oh. I don't know. Depends.'

Her mother waited for her to elaborate, but she couldn't. She didn't know quite how she felt about Spence at that moment. Yesterday, she had had enough of him, but this morning she had felt that tingle, that little zing of electricity that kept her going back for more.

'I must show you the garden. Will you look at that? The dormice have eaten all the honeysuckle!'

As her mum showed her a panoramic shot of the garden, Willow heard voices and realised the boys were back from wherever they'd been.

'Got to go, Mum!'

'Okay, have a great night!'

She ran out to greet them, hugging Spence before she helped Hugo settle on the sofa. He looked like he was in pain. She went and got him his painkillers.

'Have you had much water?' she asked. He shook his head. She glanced at Spence. The thing was, he was very willing to help, but he could be a bit dense when it came to anticipating other people's needs. You had to tell him what you wanted.

'Here.' She poured Hugo a pint of water from a large bottle. 'You really do need to drink.'

She turned to Spence. 'What have you guys been up to, anyway? Where's Josh?'

'He said something about playing tennis with a girl.'

'Elizaveta.' Hugo chimed in.

Willow raised an eyebrow. 'Can Josh play tennis?'

Hugo shrugged. 'Who cares? She can teach him.'

'Who is this Elizaveta?'

'I saw him talking to some girl the other day.' Spence said. 'She had really long hair.'

'I think I know the one you mean,' Willow said.

She and Spence settled on the chairs next to Hugo.

'So how was your day?' Spence asked.

She told them what had happened in Sozapol. Spence looked concerned.

'People drive so fast here.'

'Some people drive fast back at home, too,' Hugo said.

'Not like this.' Willow shuddered at the memory. 'It was like the car was aimed at us.'

'What did the driver look like?' Hugo asked.

'I don't know. It all happened so fast.'

Spence put his arm around her and pulled her towards him. She felt herself melt. It felt good to be back here with him. She felt safe.

'I'd better get ready if we're going out for dinner. Is Josh meeting us?'

Spence and Hugo looked at each other. 'He didn't say.'

She went into the bedroom and texted Josh. Flicking through her holiday dresses, she threw on the first one she could find and added a bit of lipstick. A glance in the mirror told her she had achieved the perfect bedhead look, so no need to mess with her hair.

She stepped out into the living room and found Hugo watching some kind of wrestling match on TV.

'I don't feel like coming out,' he said. 'Would you mind bringing me back some food?'

'What would you like?'

'Just get me whatever you're having. You've got good taste.'

She smiled. 'Okay. Can I get you anything before we go?'

He looked a bit awkward. 'Can you help me to the toilet?'

'No problem.'

She gestured for Spence to come and help too, because it was quite a job to get Hugo to his feet.

It couldn't be much fun, being stuck with a broken leg so far away from home. She wondered if they should ring his parents and ask them to come and get him. But when it came down to it, it was Hugo's call.

They went to Mehana, but Willow didn't have much appetite after her big lunch. Or was it just that she was craving something more familiar? With a jolt, she realised she was feeling homesick for her mum's potato and leek pie. It felt like ages since she had last tasted it.

She gave herself a shake. She was being ridiculous. There were only a few more days left of the holiday. She had the rest of her life to eat her mum's pie. She checked her messages. Josh hadn't even bothered to reply to her text. He must be having too much fun with Elizaveta.

Once they'd finished eating, they had a drink at the bar. Willow's eyes flicked between the other patrons. They were mostly locals or Romanians, a few Italians too, judging from the languages she could hear. She was aware of a man looking at her for a little too long. Was his interest purely the obvious, or was there something more sinister in that look? Spence took her hand and held it tight, but he didn't say anything and he didn't react. She smiled at him.

'What do you want to do tomorrow? I was thinking we should maybe go and explore a bit more. This area is so beautiful and I feel like we've barely scratched the surface. There are some easy coastal walks we could do, and I read about a pink lake in one of the guide books. That might be interesting.'

'We should come back here again,' he said. 'Just you and me. We could hire a car next time, drive along the coast a bit. I'd love to see some of the street art in Sofia.'

'Yeah, that might be cool.'

'Do you want to stay out longer?' he asked. Tiana and Lia were planning to go on to one of the clubs.

She shook her head, causing her ponytail to sway. 'I've got leftovers for Hugo,' she said, indicating the Tupperware box on the table in front of her.

He clenched his jaw, digging his teeth into the soft flesh of his lower lip until a small bead of blood formed.

'You know what I think?' he said, leaning closer. 'I think you like looking after him. I think you're enjoying it a bit too much.'

Her anger sizzled like meat on a spit. The sound of ice clinking in glasses and the chatter of their friends faded away as she stared back at him.

'You need to take a look in the mirror. If you want to have any sort of future with me, you need to grow up and stop being such a damn baby.'

Everyone went silent, as if she had smashed a plate.

Spence drew back, his bloody lip trembling violently.

'Sorry,' she said, pushing her drink away. She grabbed her bag and stormed off, tears glistening in her eyes. She didn't even know where she was going. Back to the villa, she supposed.

Her skin prickled with unease as she hurried away. She had the distinct feeling of being watched, and her heart raced with fear, amplified by the rustling of leaves in the wind. She knew it was possible Spence was following her, but she couldn't bring herself to turn around and confirm it. The thought of facing him again made her stomach twist in painful knots.

It was only when she reached the villa that she realised she had left Hugo's dinner at the bar. He was asleep anyway. She got a blanket and covered him with it. His long eyelashes fluttered slightly. His lips parted. She watched for a moment, then headed to the kitchen to make herself a cup of tea. It was ridiculous what Spence had said. She couldn't stand Hugo. He got right on her last nerve, always had. There was no way in hell she had feelings for him.

She picked up a book and tried to read but she couldn't get into it, so she set it down in favour of one of the many tourist guides lying around the room. She flicked through it, noting information about the various hidden haunts. Devil's Throat Cave. That sounded cool, but a bit too far to visit. The harbour was close by, though. Perhaps they could take a boat tour? Then again, maybe not. Knowing her friends, someone would probably fall out.

IT WAS late by the time Spence arrived home, supported by Tiana and Lia. They brought him into her room where he flopped face down on the bed.

He stank of alcohol, his clothes were slick with sweat, and he immediately started snoring.

'Hey, where am I supposed to sleep?'

'You can have Hugo's bed,' Tiana said. 'He's still on the sofa.'

Yeah. She could just imagine what Spence would make of that.

'What are you going to do about him?' Tiana asked.

Willow shrugged. She didn't really know. When she was with Spence, she felt like a caged bird. But every time she came close to getting out, she thought of all the happy memories they'd shared, of all the lovely things he had done for her. All the romantic dinners, the poems and love notes.

Tiana was still looking at her, waiting. 'It's complicated.'

They all walked out into the hallway.

'Hey, have you seen Josh?'

They shook their heads.

She checked her phone again, but there were no new messages. She had to assume Josh was still out with Elizaveta.

She should probably just go to bed. Josh was a big boy. He could take care of himself.

All the same, it nagged.

She went into Josh and Hugo's room and lay down on her brother's bed. She played on her phone for a bit and then dozed off. She was woken by the sun streaming in through the windows, burning her retinas.

No Josh, then. If he had arrived in the night, he could have slept in Hugo's empty bed. She got up and checked the living room, just in case. Hugo was still out cold, but Josh was nowhere to be seen. She looked at her phone and groaned as she saw she had run out of charge. She went into the kitchen and plugged it in while she made herself a cup of tea. Surely, if he was spending the night with Elizaveta, he would have had the decency to let her know. But as her phone pinged back to life, she saw that there were no messages. She clicked her tongue. Even Josh wasn't this inconsiderate. What if something had happened to him?

CHAPTER FOURTEEN
WILLOW

Friday

Willow drank three cups of tea before everybody else got up. She woke Hugo and asked him to check his phone. And then Lia, Spence and Tiana. Nobody had heard from Josh.

She walked down to the pool. Kelly was just opening the kiosk, beginning her daily ritual of cleaning the coffee machines and wiping down counters while her assistant put out the sun loungers.

'Have you seen my brother?' Willow asked. 'You know, blond hair, blue eyes.'

'I could hardly miss him,' Kelly said with a laugh. 'But no, I haven't seen him this morning. Sorry.'

Willow swallowed. 'What about Elizaveta? Do you know her? He said he was with her?'

Kelly nodded. 'Yeah, she comes here to swim occasionally. But I haven't seen her.'

'She's the girl with the really long hair right?'

'Yes, that's her. Don't tell me they've run off together?'

'Josh wouldn't run off,' Willow said grimly. 'I'm getting

The Beach

really worried. Can you tell me where the police station is? If he doesn't come back soon, I'm going to report him missing.'

Kelly's face grew serious. 'It's down near the market. Behind the flower shop. But surely he's just off having fun, sowing his wild oats?'

Willow shuddered at the phrase. 'That's just it. I don't know what he's doing. He hasn't been in touch.'

'Well, that's boys for you, I'm afraid. My brothers were exactly the same.'

Willow clenched and unclenched her fists. There was something about this conversation that was winding her up. Without another word, she stalked off, down the footpath towards the town.

'Have you tried calling the hospitals?' Kelly called after her. 'Perhaps he's got drunk again?'

Willow hadn't realised that was public knowledge. But surely Josh wouldn't be so stupid? He had been careful not to go overboard since that incident. She kept walking, trying to work out the tension in her body. She was probably overreacting. Josh was fine. After all, he was a grown up. In fact, it was his birthday, she suddenly realised. He was eighteen today. His birthday, and he hadn't come home.

Just a couple more hours, she told herself. He'll come home with his tail between his legs, embarrassed, hungover. Or else all loved up and dreamy after a night with that girl. We'll all laugh about it. It will be fine.

She walked on, taking the path that led down to the beach. Dark clouds loomed on the horizon and red flags flapped violently in the wind. The deserted shore was strewn with debris, and the waves crashed against the rocks with such force that she thought they might shatter. All along the boardwalk, the cafes and shops were shuttered, and Josh was nowhere to be seen.

Her phone pinged. She grabbed it out of her pocket.

There was a message:

. . .

Sorry, my phone was out of charge. Call off the search party!

She let out a big whoop of relief and sent back an instant reply:

Happy birthday, Loser!

She waited, but he didn't rise to the bait. She would have liked to speak to him, but obviously he was busy. She sent him another text:

Don't forget to call Mum!

She walked back up to the villa, relieved that everything was okay. Was this how her mum felt when she and Josh went out at night? But she was never this inconsiderate. She had got drunk a couple of times. But she always called her mother. She never left her hanging. It was out of character for Josh too. This girl must have really got under his skin.

Spence was in the kitchen when she came back. His shoulders were hunched, face steeped with regret.

'I was an idiot,' he said, eyes downcast. 'I don't know what came over me. I just felt such a deep sense of loss. I know I'm losing you.'

'You're not losing me.'

'I felt so wretched. I went to the bar and chugged down a load of Rakia.'

'How's that supposed to help?'

'Like I said, I'm an idiot.'

'Are you suffering for it?'

'Just the normal amount.'

He dared to look up at her. Those eyes were still beautiful and tender, the same eyes that had once drawn her to him. She stood stiffly in front of him. This was the part where she was supposed to put her arms around him, where the fight was supposed to bring them closer together.

'Will you be coming down to the pool?'

She turned and started searching through her things for her bikini.

'I'm still a bit fragile. Perhaps I should stay here and do a bit of writing.'

'Okay.'

She was glad he was writing. It was better for him than brooding.

AFTER A LONG, refreshing swim, she climbed out of the pool and flopped down on a sun lounger next to Hugo. He was dozing contentedly, enjoying the warmth of the sun. Shielding her eyes from the bright rays, she looked up at the villa and saw Spence on the balcony. She smiled and waved, but he didn't seem to notice her. Instead, his focus was fixed on something, or someone else. In his hands, she caught a glimmer of metallic light and realised he was using binoculars. He had them trained up on the cliffs that overlooked the sea. Perhaps he was watching the seabirds.

EVERYONE GOT DRESSED up for Josh's birthday dinner. Willow wore her favourite tartan dress, and Tiana put on a skin-tight cat suit, and used make up to create heavy, smoky eyes.

'When's he coming?' she kept asking, as Willow styled her

hair.

'I don't know,' Willow said. It was almost time to go. 'I suppose he'll meet us there.'

She put the finishing touches to her own make up and texted Josh to remind him she had booked the restaurant for eight o'clock.

'Is he bringing Elizaveta?' Tiana asked.

'I don't know. He hasn't said anything.'

'Yeah, well, he'll be bored of her soon enough.'

Tiana checked her lip gloss in the mirror and sauntered out. Once again, Willow was left wondering why she was so hung up on her brother. Tiana was confident, outgoing, and attractive. She could have her pick of the men if she chose, but she always seemed to want what she couldn't have. Perhaps that was the attraction.

THEY WALKED DOWN to the restaurant, with Hugo hobbling along behind them. Willow patted her handbag to check her gift was still there. She had saved all summer and bought Josh an Apple Watch. She had wanted to get him something special because he was a good brother, really. And she was excited that he was finally eighteen. He had always resented the fact that she was that bit older than him. She had been allowed into nightclubs first, allowed to drink legally before him, even allowed to drive before him. All the firsts. And now he had finally caught her up. No one was more excited about that than her.

As they were shown to their table, their group was the object of curious glances from other diners. She had phoned ahead to let them know this was to be a special birthday celebration, but they seemed to have misunderstood her message.

They had decorated their table with colourful streamers and balloons and there was a sparkling gold table cloth. Hugo was in hysterics at the Thomas the Tank Engine napkins.

The Beach

'Shush,' she warned him. 'They've gone to a lot of trouble!'

They sat down, leaving the place at the head of the table free for Josh. Hugo reached for his silver party hat and put it on his head, tucking the elastic string under his chin.

'Haven't worn one of these in years!'

Spence glowered at him across the table, then seemed to catch himself and looked down at his plate. Hugo didn't even seem to notice. He boldly ordered his drink in Bulgarian, but from the expressions on the waiter's face, he couldn't understand a word of what he was saying.

Willow reached for the cocktail menu and found the exact drink she was going to buy Josh. A bright purple one with little sunglasses on it. He was going to love it.

She looked around the table. Everyone was fizzing with anticipation.

She couldn't wait to see her brother's face when he saw his fantastic apple watch. She couldn't wait for the night to begin.

Her phone rang.

'Hi Mum. We're at the restaurant.'

She turned the phone around so everyone could wave, then she brought it back to face her.

'We're just waiting for Josh now. He's met a girl. She's probably doing her hair. Or his.'

Her mum laughed. 'Sounds like our Josh. Are you still having a good time?'

'Brilliant!' She almost choked on her words, but she didn't want to think about the week she had had. She wanted to focus on tonight, on Josh's birthday. This was the highlight of the week. This would make it all worthwhile.

'It all looks amazing. Wish I was there.'

'We're going to do it all again when we get home, and we'll have to take Josh for a pint at our local.'

'That'll be lovely.'

She checked the door to make sure Josh hadn't arrived

while she was on the phone.

'There's a cake,' she said, moving the phone towards it. 'It's got Peppa Pig on it.'

Her mum giggled. 'Brilliant. He's going to love it.'

WILLOW SET DOWN HER PHONE. Spence draped his arm across the back of her chair. He kept dotting little kisses along her collar bone. It made her feel uncomfortable. She got the sense that he was only doing it to claim her, to show she was his.

Hugo was sitting on the other side of the table, next to Lia. She looked over and wondered what they were talking about. Lia spoke in such a soft voice, you had to listen carefully to catch her words. Whatever she was saying, she had Hugo's attention. He was nodding gravely, brows knitted with concern.

The waiting staff brought out some nibbles.

'I'm hungry,' Hugo said loudly. 'When are we going to order?'

Willow exchanged a glance with Spence. 'I don't want to order till Josh gets here. He's the guest of honour.'

'How about we get starters?' Hugo suggested. 'Something to keep us going.'

Willow nodded. The waiter appeared at their table as if by magic. People started calling out their orders and before she knew it, they had ordered every damned starter on the menu.

'Can you call Josh?' she asked Hugo. She was aware that her brother saw her as a bit of a nag. But Hugo was his best friend. He wouldn't ignore him, surely? Obligingly, Hugo picked up his phone. He stared at it for a few minutes, then shook his head.

'Maybe he's on his way? The signals are not so good in the mountains.'

She looked at him sharply. 'What would he be doing in the mountains? Did he say something to you?'

'Not a word. But we were talking to Kelly at the kiosk the other day and she mentioned the mountains were quite beautiful and Josh seemed interested. Perhaps Elizaveta has taken him sightseeing. What else would they be doing all this time?'

Tiana rolled her eyes at that and slammed down her glass of wine. 'He was only supposed to be playing tennis.'

'What if they've broken down somewhere?' Lia said. 'He might need help.'

'Hard to know where to start, given that he hasn't said where he was going,' Spence said. 'I'm betting he's still here in Paradise Palms somewhere, making the most of his birthday.'

Willow rang Josh again when the starters arrived and left him an irate message.

'We're all waiting for you. Get your birthday butt down here pronto, or I'll set Mum on you.'

'I've been thinking,' Spence said, picking at a piece of cheese.

'Yes?'

'You know Tom's going to get me an apprenticeship at his work?'

'You never said?'

'Yeah, well, I wanted to keep my options open, but now I'm thinking I should just go for it. It will be good to be earning a steady wage. Better than what I earn at the shop, anyway.'

She nodded. 'Makes sense.'

'And then we could get a flat together?'

Her jaw slackened, her mind racing with conflicting emotions.

'What, you don't want to?'

'I…I don't want to rent. I'm saving up to buy my own place.'

He leaned back in his chair, studying her face. 'Do you really think that, or are you just trying to fob me off?'

'I'm not like that. You know I'm not.'

But he was bang on the money. He was the one putting her on the spot, pressuring her.

The waiter returned to their table, the wheels of his trolley squeaking as he pushed it towards them. Willow breathed in the heavenly smell of grilled meat and mixed spices as he unloaded it all onto their table. She suspected Hugo had ordered it all; meat wrapped in vine leaves, mixed grill, and the inevitable Shopska salad, not to mention a fresh round of drinks.

She smiled at Hugo across the table because the food really was delicious. The drinks kept flowing, and each time she put down her glass, it was topped up again.

Finally, the waiter returned to their table and said in a whisper:

'Is it time for the cake yet?'

Willow sighed. 'No, the birthday boy is not here yet.'

The waiter looked around at all the empty plates. 'Oh! Some more drinks then?'

She nodded wearily. They were all getting drunk and there was no way of stopping it. She couldn't blame her friends. Josh was incredibly late.

'Where the hell is he?'

A drunk Tiana winked at her. 'I've got him tied up in my wardrobe.'

'Not funny.'

Hugo banged his spoon against his glass. 'Everyone, Lia's got an announcement.'

Lia immediately went red. 'Not here, Hugo. It's not the time.'

'No, go on,' Willow said, studying her friend's face.

Lia looked across the table at her, then darted a look at Tiana.

'I've been offered a place at Sunderland University and I've decided to take it.'

'Sunderland?' Willow said, stunned. 'I thought you wanted

to go to Reading?'

'Well I'm going to Sunderland.'

Tiana googled it on her phone. She looked up sharply. 'That's almost three hundred miles away!'

'I know.'

They all looked at each other.

'Well, good luck, I guess,' Willow said, slowly.

Just then, a burst of loud music sounded from outside. She recognised one of Josh's favourite songs. They all sat up straight as the double doors were thrown open.

'Way to make an entrance!' Tiana called out.

Willow leaned forward eagerly. It wasn't Josh, but a tall brunette wearing a skimpy bra top and a long, glittery skirt.

The woman strode into the restaurant, her heels clicking on the tiled floor.

'Where's the birthday boy?' she called out.

'Oh god, kill me now,' Willow said, shielding her eyes.

'He's not here,' Tiana said, looking annoyed.

The smile slipped. 'Look mate, I've only got half an hour, then I've got to get to my next gig.'

'You might as well go ahead,' Hugo said. His eyes met Spence's. 'Since we've already paid and all.'

Spence nodded. With a sigh, she began to belly dance.

Tiana and Lia were giggling like crazy as she did her thing, moving her hips in a hypnotic dance and shaking her booty. Then she turned round and jiggled her breasts. The restaurant grew quiet as everyone watched. Even the waiters stopped serving.

Belatedly, Spence thought to film the performance for Josh.

'You organised this?' she whispered.

'Not me, Hugo. I chipped in towards it, for his birthday present. What a waste.'

The belly dancer finished with a flourish and everyone clapped and cheered. Then Hugo bought her a cocktail, which she chugged down in a few gulps. She left quietly, her butt wiggling behind her as she walked out the door. So that was it. Josh had missed his birthday belly dance.

'You should have told him there was going to be a dancer,' Willow said. 'I bet he wouldn't have been late then.'

'We did drop a few subtle hints,' Hugo said.

'And a few not-so-subtle ones,' Spence added.

She looked at him curiously. 'Did you?'

He nodded.

She rang him one more time, and one more time she got through to his voice mail.

She got up and followed the dancer outside. She could see her standing on the pavement, taking a long drag of a cigarette.

Willow pulled out her phone and found a picture of Josh.

'This is what he looks like, my brother.'

'Very nice.'

'Yeah, well, if you see him out tonight, can you tell him to call me? My name's Willow.'

The belly dancer exhaled, blowing smoke in Willow's face.

'I'm not your babysitter. If your brother has missed his party, he must have had a better offer.'

Bitch.

Willow headed back inside. Spence was shaking his head, but they were doing it anyway, lighting the candles on Josh's spectacular birthday cake. The lights flickered eerily in the breeze and before anyone could stop them, the waiters were singing Happy Birthday. Soon the whole restaurant was joining in. Spence was waving his arms like mad, but no one took the least bit of notice. They finished singing and everyone waited for someone to blow out the candles. Willow walked over and blew them out for her brother. The room erupted with applause. She looked up and met her friends' eyes.

Where the hell are you, Josh?

CHAPTER FIFTEEN
PATSY

Friday

Patsy fumbled with her keys and unlocked the side door, bracing herself for the chaos that usually greeted her. But this time, there was an eerie silence. She followed the trail of toys to the hallway, where she found her husband, Bill, lying at the foot of the stairs, his body covered with Willow's pink blanket. Josh's favourite teddy bear, Reggie, lay beside him on the floor. Josh sat close to his dad, updating him on the latest episode of Thomas the Tank Engine, whilst Willow tried to feed him a cup of tea, most of which had spilled down his shirt.

She dropped her bags and collapsed onto the floor beside her children, hugging them both fiercely as tears streamed down her face. Her heart shattered as she realised that Bill must have been lying there for much of the weekend. There was no colour left in his cheeks, and his body was already stiff with rigor mortis. She couldn't bear the thought that she hadn't been there to save him, or to help her children deal with the most harrowing event of their young lives.

. . .

SHE JERKED upright on the sofa. She must have fallen asleep. It had been a long time since she had had that dream. Well, not a dream, really. A tragic, excruciating memory.

She looked at her watch. She had waited all afternoon for Josh to call. Even though Willow had said he was busy with some girl, she had still thought he would phone her on his birthday. After all, she was his mum. He must have known she had been thinking of him.

Her guess was that he had had too much to drink. That sounded about right. He was probably too drunk to be put on the phone. She recalled his sixteenth birthday when he had gone out with friends and got absolutely slaughtered. Willow had tried to cover up for him, but in the end, she had brought him home, and Patsy had had to look after him. Still, she felt sad. She had known Josh would be away for his birthday. She had been ready for that. She just hadn't been ready to be completely ignored.

She tapped her fingers on the table. It was almost nine. He could still ring, she supposed. Then she remembered Kelly. Kelly would find out what was going on.

'I wouldn't worry,' Kelly said when she came on the line. 'I saw them heading off to the restaurant, dressed to the nines. Are you celebrating yourself? You should be. It's a big milestone, their eighteenth. You should be having a little party of your own.'

Patsy smiled. 'I've got a friend coming over in a minute. We'll open a bottle of bubbly.'

'That's more like it. You have your own celebration. Don't worry about Josh. He'll be having a whale of a time.'

'I'm sure you're right.'

'Anyway, he'll be back home on Sunday, won't he? The holiday's nearly over.'

'Yeah, that's true. Oh, that's the doorbell now. Thanks for the chat.'

She hung up, feeling a little better. She was so fortunate to

The Beach

have found Kelly. It was so reassuring to have a little window into her children's lives.

Misha stood in the doorway, holding a bottle of champagne. They hugged, and Patsy took the bubbly into the kitchen and popped it open.

'So,' she asked, as they settled down on the sofa. 'How are you coping without your baby on his birthday?'

'Not bad, now you're here,' Patsy said, clinking her glass.

'I can't believe he's eighteen,' Misha said. 'I could have sworn he was a baby just yesterday. They both were.'

'I can't believe it either,' Patsy said. It was incredible the way time flew by. It felt like just yesterday Bill had been sitting here with baby Willow on his lap, while she nursed newborn Josh.

She looked around her empty living room. Without her kids, the house seemed so quiet. And they weren't really kids anymore. They were both grown up. She felt a lump in her throat and swallowed hard.

Misha settled on the bean bag, as she always did. She lay back and looked up at the ceiling, her cornrows dangling on the floor. She smiled contentedly and started telling Patsy about some drama that was going on at the college where she worked. She always had funny stories to tell, but Patsy wasn't really listening. She was thinking about Willow and Josh, wondering what they were doing. Was the party over now? Had they headed to the club? And what about this girl Willow had mentioned? Was it serious between her and Josh? What if it was, and she wanted him to move to Bulgaria? She didn't think she could bear it.

Misha burst out laughing. 'You're not listening to a word I've said, are you?'

Patsy flushed. 'Sorry.'

'No, that's alright. Just tell me what's going on in that brain of yours.'

So Patsy told her about how disappointed she was that Josh hadn't called. How she missed hearing from him.

'Well, they've got each other,' Misha said. 'I'm sure Willow will be keeping Josh in line.'

They poured more wine and Patsy brought up the Paradise Palms website to show Misha.

'Wow, that looks amazing. Maybe you and I could take a trip there sometime?'

Patsy smiled. She had never really thought about going away without the children. The purpose of her holidays, for so many years, had been to create memories with them.

'That sounds lovely,' she said tentatively. She tried to picture herself lounging around on a sunbed.

'We might even meet some toy boys.'

Patsy burst out laughing. The last man she had been interested in had turned out to be married, and it had put her right off relationships altogether. She was perfectly happy being on her own. But if Misha wanted to have a little fun, then good for her.

'So when will the kids be back?'

'Sunday. I've got to drive to the airport for nine.'

'Oh, that's a bit harsh for a Sunday morning. They'll owe you.'

'I'm happy to do it.'

'Course you are.'

'Have they sent you a postcard?'

'That would be nice, but no one sends postcards anymore, apparently.'

'But they've been in touch?'

'Willow has. Not a word from Josh, but I do have other sources, and they tell me that Willow's boyfriend is there with her, even though she expressly told me he wasn't going.'

Misha looked at her out of the corner of her eye. 'Hang on, wind that back a minute. What other sources?'

Patsy took a sip of wine and explained her deal with Kelly.

She thought her friend would understand, but instead, Misha's eyes grew wide.

'You've got to be bloody kidding me!'

'Why?'

'That sounds well creepy, getting some woman from the Internet to spy on your kids!'

Patsy set down her glass. 'No, she's nice. I've spoken to her on Facetime. We get on really well.'

'But you don't know her, do you? You've told her exactly where your children are. And you're trusting her to be a good person and look out for them. But Patsy, you don't know who she really is or what her intentions are. She could be anyone.'

CHAPTER SIXTEEN
WILLOW

They stayed at the table, drinking and waiting for Josh. They were so drunk, Willow wished they'd all go home. She glared at Lia. 'What are you still doing here? I thought you hated us.'

'I never said that.'

'Well, do me a favour and go back to the villa, just in case Josh is there.'

Lia stared at her. 'No.'

'What?'

'I'm sick of you telling me what to do all the time. You're so bossy. No wonder Josh didn't want to come.'

Willow stared at her for a moment, fighting the urge to slap her. Lia scraped back her chair. 'On second thoughts, I will head back. I don't want to sit here a second longer.'

'What a bitch!' Tiana said the minute she had walked out the door.

Willow looked at her. 'Did she say anything to you about going off to Sunderland?'

'Not a word. But now I think of it, she's been a bit weird all summer. Hinting that we're holding her back or something.'

Willow felt a lump in her throat. 'But we've been friends… for years. Why did she even come on the holiday if she hates us so much?'

Hugo raised his head. 'She doesn't hate you. She just wants to step out of your shadow.'

'Whatever. This is bullshit.'

She let out a puff of air. 'And where the hell is my brother?'

The waiter approached them. 'I'm sorry, but we're closing now.'

Willow nodded, swallowing her tears. It was gone midnight.

They headed back to the villa. Her heart skipped a beat when she saw the lights were on, but it was just Lia, sitting in the kitchen.

'Is he back?'

Lia shook her head.

She checked anyway, half expecting to find him passed out on the sofa, or in his bed. But there was no sign of him. She paced around the living room.

'I can't believe he did this to us. He knew that we were having his birthday dinner tonight. Why would he miss it?'

'I don't know,' Hugo said, easing himself onto the sofa.

'It's really weird, isn't it?' Spence said. 'Do you think he's alright?'

'That girl has done something to him,' Tiana said.

They all looked at each other and Willow was struck by the biggest bolt of dread she had ever felt in her life. Josh had never fallen for anyone, not completely. They were always more interested in him than he was in them. He had never experienced that all-consuming passion that other teenagers went through. It was hard to believe Elizaveta was the exception.

She put her shoes back on.

'Where are you going?' Spence asked.

'Out. I'm looking for Josh.'

He nodded. 'I'll come with you.'

Soon they were outside, walking through the pool area, looking at the stillness of the water. They kept walking, down to the beach. Willow went into the bar, while Spence spoke to a couple of people he recognised.

Willow showed the pizza guy Josh's picture. She gave him her number and he smiled like she was asking him for a date. She could just imagine how Spence would react to that.

She left quickly and they walked into the town. There were lots of people out that night. The two clubs looked quite busy. They went into each of them, but there was no sign of Josh.

She asked the door men. They all knew who Elizaveta was.

'She does come in here,' one of them said. 'But can't say I've seen her.'

Willow nodded. 'If you do see her, can you give her my number?'

She scribbled it down for him, and walked out onto the street where the air was cooler.

They kept walking along the strip. At the very last bar, right on the water's edge, she saw a girl with waist length hair and a little snub nose. Elizaveta. She hurried over to her. She was sitting with three other girls, drinking cocktails.

Willow tapped her on the shoulder.

'Hi, I'm Josh's sister. Where is he?'

Elizaveta blinked at her 'Who?'

Willow bit back her impatience. 'Josh.'

She showed Elizaveta a photo on her phone.

'Ah, now I remember,' she said with a smile. 'He is very good looking. How can I forget?'

'So where is he?'

'I don't know.'

Willow blinked. 'Well, when did you last see him? After tennis?'

Elizaveta rubbed her throat and looked at her friends.

'I only met your brother once, down on the beach. Sure, he was nice. I gave him my number, but he never called. I was a little disappointed, to be honest. I thought we could have some fun. When you see him, tell him I'm waiting.'

Willow swallowed hard. 'He said he was with you.'

Elizaveta shook her head. 'I really don't understand. I haven't seen him. Must be some other girl.'

'She's been with us all day,' one of her friends said. The others nodded.

Willow grabbed onto the table. The world was spinning.

Where the hell was Josh?

CHAPTER SEVENTEEN
WILLOW

Her heart raced as she stumbled away into the cool night air. She leaned heavily against Spence, gasping for breath as she tried to calm herself down.

'Hey, is that Tiana?' Spence said.

Willow followed his gaze. Sure enough, there she was, staggering drunkenly along the beach.

'Did you find him?' Tiana asked.

'Just Elizaveta. She says she hasn't seen him.'

'Lying skank!'

Tiana followed her gaze and stormed over to Elizaveta's table.

Willow looked at Spence. 'Oh shit!'

Tiana didn't waste any time. She grabbed hold of Elizaveta's hair and she was yanking her back from the table. Elizaveta's friends were trying to help, but they were no match for a drunk Tiana.

'Tell me where he is!'

'Tiana, stop! She doesn't know anything.'

Spence stepped up and between the two of them, they managed to yank Tiana off her.

The Beach

'So sorry,' Willow said.

'You're crazy!' Elizaveta shouted at Tiana. She glared at Willow. 'Keep your mad dog under control or you'll all be pissing gas.'

Tiana made a move to have another go, but Spence kept a hold of her. 'I'm calling you a taxi.'

'Why? I want to find Josh!'

'You're going to land yourself in jail at the rate you're going.'

They sat down on a bench and Willow pulled out her phone. She read Josh's last text. Now she looked at it closely, it didn't even sound like Josh. Too brief. Too business like. Where were the emojis he loved to use? Where was the follow up? Because when Josh sent a text, there was almost always a follow up. He texted like he spoke, rapid fire, one thought after another. This text was nothing like that.

Because it wasn't from him.

She looked at Spence. 'I think someone's taken him.'

'What do you want to do?'

'We need to find the police station. It's not far from here.'

'What about Tiana?'

Tiana lifted her head. 'I'm fine.'

Willow looked up and saw Kelly walking towards them.

'Oh dear,' she said, looking at Tiana. 'You're looking a bit worse for wear.'

'We still can't find Josh,' Willow said, blinking back tears. 'Spence and I are going to go to the police station. Will it be open at this time?'

Kelly frowned. 'I'm not sure. Maybe.'

Spence scratched his head. 'It would be really great if you could see Tiana back to the villa for us.'

'Of course. No problem.'

'Hey, I can walk myself back!' Tiana objected.

'With Josh missing, I'd rather you had someone with you,' Spence said.

Kelly nodded, 'I quite agree. Safety in numbers and all that.'

'Thanks so much.'

Willow smiled awkwardly as Kelly and Tiana walked off. There was something ever so slightly off about Kelly, but she had saved their lives once, so she must be basically alright. Besides, she really needed to report Josh missing.

Spence gave her his arm and guided her forward, his touch warm and reassuring. She squinted through the haze of tears as they looked for the police station. It was exactly as Kelly had said, tucked behind the market square.

As they approached, she saw that the building was in darkness. Panic surged through her.

'Now what?'

She peered through the windows and got a glimpse of the inside. Not a soul to be seen.

'We'll have to ring them,' Spence said.

'On what number?'

'I don't know. We should have asked Kelly.'

'Let's head back to the villa. We'll figure it out there.'

She felt like she was walking through a fog, uncertain of what to do next. As they rounded the corner, she saw a man she recognised, though it took her a moment to realise where she knew him from. He was the man who propped up the bar at the Golden Hour. It was strange to see him out of context.

'Something is wrong?' he asked, looking from her to Spence.

She realised she had tears in her eyes. She took a step towards him.

'My brother is missing. No one's seen him since yesterday.'

He wiped his hand on his vest. 'Your brother?'

'Yes. Can you help?'

'Maybe I can. Come with me.'

'Where? Where are we going?'

'We need to go to my friend's house.'

'And they will help?'

He stopped and looked at her, seeming to realise she required more explanation.

'I'm a policeman. I mean, I'm off duty right now, but I know where to find my colleagues.'

Her heart beat a little faster. 'Thank you! Thank you so much!'

The tears were streaming now, and there was nothing she could do to stop them.

He patted her shoulder. 'Try not to worry.'

'But what if something's happened to him?'

She had a flash of the car speeding towards them in Sozopol, Hugo's accident, Tiana's fall from the balcony.

'Someone will have seen something. This is not such a big place. You can't sneeze without somebody seeing.'

He glanced at his watch, and then back at them. 'Oh, and my name is Radoslav. I'd tell you my last name, but you wouldn't be able to pronounce it.'

He let out a low chuckle.

'Thank you, Radoslav. I'm Willow and this is…'

'No need. I already know who you are.'

She exchanged a glance with Spence, who smiled uneasily.

Radoslav was still talking as he led them away from the square. He walked unsteadily, stumbling a bit. He headed up the hill, and Willow faltered a little. She could see the doubt on Spence's face. Then he gave a little shrug and they forged ahead.

Radoslav kept walking, then suddenly turned round and looked at them, waving at them to hurry up. They passed a large, beautiful house that overlooked the sea. The lights were on, but he kept going, until they came to more houses. Smaller, shabbier ones. More like outbuildings than proper houses. When they reached the last house, he stopped. Wooden planks covered one of the windows, and there was a sign with exclamation marks on it, but it was all in Cyrillic, so Willow had no idea what it said. There were several cars parked in the driveway, and a couple of motorbikes. She heard barking as they walked up the path. Radoslav pushed the flimsy door open and entered without knocking. It swung shut behind him.

They heard him speaking in rapid Bulgarian to whoever was inside.

Spence looked at Willow. 'What now? Do we follow him?'

Willow swallowed. 'I suppose...'

She pushed open the door and blinked into the dim light. Radoslav stood at a table where a group of men sat playing cards. Most of them were smoking, cigarettes dangling from their lips. She stood off to the side, shifting her weight from one foot to the other while he talked to them in Bulgarian. The men looked at her, unsmiling. There were big men, scruffy looking, wearing vests and shorts that revealed their hairy legs. She wondered if they were all policemen. She looked around, but there was no sign of the dogs she had heard. Perhaps they were out the back.

She heard a sound behind her and saw Spence step into the room. He came over to her, looking distinctly uncomfortable.

'I'm not sure about this,' he said in a low voice.

'Me either.'

From the kitchen emerged a small, hunched woman balancing a tray in her gnarled hands. The tray held an assortment of dried fruits, sundried tomatoes, and slices of cured meat. She gawped at Spence as if he was some exotic specimen. He made the mistake of smiling, and she tsked at the gap in his teeth.

'Sit. Eat.'

There were two stools under the table. They pulled them out and sat down. Politely, Spence picked up a piece of meat and chewed it. Satisfied, the old woman disappeared back to the kitchen. The men had abandoned their card game and were now looking at their phones. They seemed to be planning a search. Radoslav had a map out, and one of the others was looking at a weather app.

Spence was still chewing his piece of meat.

'I think this is horse,' he said, pushing it around in his mouth.

Willow ignored him and focused on the men. It was so frustrating not being able to understand what was being said. Finally, Radoslav turned to look at her.

'Right then, we will take your statement properly tomorrow, but in the meantime, tell us everywhere your brother has been since he's arrived here. Everyone he has spoken to, and we'll put the word out, see if anyone has seen him.'

He handed her a piece of paper and a pen, and she started writing.

'Do you think all this is legit?' Spence murmured in her ear. 'I mean, how do we even know these people are police? They could be anybody.'

'I think we have to trust them,' she whispered back. 'What choice do we have?'

She looked at the men again. If she had spotted them in the street, she would not have pegged them for police. If anything, she would have said they looked like criminals, with their scarred faces and stubbly chins. And if they truly were police, then they must be poorly paid, judging by the state of their clothes. But what did all that matter if they were going to help her find Josh?

It was around two in the morning by the time they headed back to the villa. The others were waiting up for them. She updated them, and Tiana broke down in tears.

'I knew something was wrong. How could we sit in that restaurant, eating when Josh is missing?'

Lia slipped an arm around Tiana as she sobbed. Hugo just sat there, looking down at his knees.

Willow walked past them all and headed for her bedroom. Spence followed her and they both flopped down on the bed.

'What if we don't find him, Spence? I can't go home without him. I just can't.'

'We'll stay as long as it takes,' he said firmly.

She nodded, glad to have him on side. She thought about what to do next. It was going to break her heart, but she couldn't put it off any longer. It was time to call her mum.

CHAPTER EIGHTEEN
PATSY

Patsy didn't like the look Misha was giving her. She had been so certain that Kelly's offer was the answer to all her worries. She hadn't even thought to google her. She had taken her at her word, because she had seemed so normal, so down to earth. After that first meeting over Facetime, she had let all her barriers down.

She typed Kelly's name into google and gasped as she dredged up a news article. It wasn't a recent story. The events in it had taken place over ten years ago. But it hit home, all the same.

'Look at this,' she said, hands shaking slightly as she showed it to Misha. Her friend leaned over and they both scanned the text.

Ten years ago, a nineteen-year-old British man called Pierce had fallen from a balcony and drowned in the swimming pool at the Paradise Palms resort. His heartbroken mother, Kelly Armitage, had flown out to Bulgaria to retrieve his body. There was an inquest, but nobody was held liable for the death. Pierce had had a lot to drink, and drugs were found in his system too. His judgement had clearly been impaired. Unfortunately, his friends were all at the beach or else asleep at the time and nobody had noticed he was missing until his body was discovered at the bottom of the swimming pool. Kelly was heartbroken. Pierce was her only child.

'And now she works there,' Patsy said incredulously. 'But why? Why would you want to stay in a place that holds such tragic memories?'

'Maybe she feels close to him there,' Misha said. 'It makes a bit more sense now, this teen minding service of hers. No one was there for her son. But she's there, looking out for others.'

Patsy scrolled back and looked at the picture of Pierce. He was so young and handsome. He had lovely blue eyes that seemed to shine through the screen.

'That poor woman! What a tragedy.'

Misha put down her glass. 'I still think she could be dodgy, offering to watch your kids like that. I really don't like it.'

Patsy pressed her lips together. Misha wasn't a mother. She didn't understand how desperate it could be, the urge to keep your children safe, to protect them.

Misha left a little while later and they agreed to speak the following week. Patsy trudged up the stairs, pausing at the top to listen to the silence. They would be home soon, she told herself. Just two more sleeps.

As she drifted off, she had a random memory of a young Josh spying on her, watching her from under the table. She had pretended not to notice him as she did the washing up. Then she had heard a little giggle. She had turned to see his sweet little face peeking out and she couldn't resist scooping him up in her arms for a hug. She and Josh had always had that sort of relationship. Close and tactile. He reminded her so much of Bill.

Somewhere, a sheep was beating. The noise was repetitive and insistent and really quite annoying. She turned over and tried to get away from it, but the sheep kept going, bleating and bleating in her right ear, until she realised she was in bed.

The Beach

She blinked at her phone. It was ringing. She squinted at the digital clock. It was midnight, so it must be about 2AM in Bulgaria. She grabbed it.

'What's wrong?'

She knew before Willow could even get the words out that it was Josh.

Something had happened to him. Something so terrible that it couldn't wait for the morning.

'Tell me!'

Whatever it was, she wouldn't be shocked. She had waited Josh's whole life for something terrible to happen to him. He was too perfect, too beautiful, her baby boy. Whatever dark scenario had unfolded, she had already seen it, already enacted it, in her mind's eye. That's what you did when you loved someone so fiercely that every fibre of your being depended on it.

Willow was silent for a moment. 'I don't know where he is. He met a girl, and we thought he was with her. But he wasn't. She hasn't seen him. I think…I think someone's taken him.'

Patsy's chest pounded faster and faster. It felt like it was gaining speed, like a ball rolling down a hill.

'Have you contacted the police?'

'Yes.'

She thought for a moment. 'I need you to listen very carefully. There's a woman there, a woman that runs a kiosk. Her name is Kelly.'

'Yes, I've met her.'

'Go and see her. She might be able to help. And hang tight, love. I'm going to head to the airport. I'll get the first plane out there. I'll be there as soon as I can.'

'Okay. I love you Mum.'

'I love you too. Try not to worry.'

CHAPTER NINETEEN
KELLY

Saturday

It's the first thing I see when I wake up. The posts on Facebook. Everyone is getting into a frenzy over the missing English boy.

Straight away, I ring his mother, but she doesn't answer. Either she's still asleep or she's on her way out here, dropping everything just like I did all those years ago. I will never forget that feeling, when those pathetic friends of Pierce's finally got up the nerve to call me. His body was already cold by then, already chilling in the morgue. They had me do the formal identification. They told me I didn't have to view the actual body, that I could look at a photograph instead. But I had to see him in the flesh because otherwise I would never have believed it. I remember how well he looked. That was the thing that shocked me. He wasn't so different. My Pierce was still in there. I was sure of it.

I only intended to stay a few days. Long enough to make the arrangements and deal with the paperwork. But there was something about this place, this Paradise Palms. I felt as though as long as I was here, we could still be together. I sensed his soul in the air around me. Better still, I could hear his voice. He whispered to me.

Don't leave me, Mum.
You need to stay here.
You need to make it right.

So THAT's what I've been doing with my life ever since. I continue to see him, to hear him. His voice has grown stronger. No more a whisper, more like a hidden microphone in my ear. It was Pierce who told me I needed to keep a closer eye on this group. Especially on the boy. I don't always understand the words Pierce uses. The things he asks me to do, but I trust my son with all my heart, and I will never let him down again. I wasn't here when he needed me, but I'm as sure as hell here now.

CHAPTER TWENTY
WILLOW

Saturday

Kelly handed out cups of coffee and bottles of mineral water as the volunteers gathered down by the pool. There must have been as many as fifty people, a mix of locals and tourists who had come forward to volunteer their time. Willow looked around the group, her eyes welling up at the generosity of all these people who didn't know her or Josh but simply wanted to help.

'Could he have gone to the caves?' Lia asked. 'He was harping on about them at the beginning of the week.'

Willow shook her head. Josh had been interested in visiting the caves but they were over four hours' drive so she had talked him out of it. And there was no way he would have gone ahead on his own without letting anyone know.

'What if someone offered to take him and that's where he is?'

She turned and waved to Radoslav. He looked very different today, neatly shaved and in uniform. She repeated Lia's question.

The Beach

'I'll ring and check,' he said. 'I can contact the local taxi companies and the personnel at the caves.'

'Thank you.'

Radoslav clapped his hands and began talking in rapid Bulgarian. Then he switched to English.

'Good morning, everyone. First, I want to thank you all for coming out today to help in the search for Joshua Spicer, known as Josh. Your help means a lot to Josh's family and to all of us involved in this effort.

Before we begin, I want to remind everyone that safety is our top priority. Please stay with your assigned groups and within your designated search areas. Be mindful of your surroundings and please avoid taking unnecessary risks. If you encounter any issues, contact the command centre immediately. We will provide each group with a map and a contact number.

You should all have received a copy of the report about Josh, which includes pictures of him. We believe he was wearing a grey t-shirt and brown or black shorts and possibly a baseball cap on the day he went missing. Look for any signs of Josh, or personal belongings that might belong to him. If you find anything significant, please mark the location on your map without disturbing it. Remember, your efforts today can make a crucial difference. Thank you again for your help and let's all do our best to bring Josh back safely. Now, if nobody has any questions, we will split you into groups.'

Willow was put into a group with Spence. Tiana and Lia were in another group. She turned and looked at Hugo, who was sitting on a sun lounger by the pool.

'I feel bad that I can't help,' he said.

'It's not your fault. But perhaps you could subtly question the other holidaymakers? We haven't got much of a timeline so far. Someone might have seen him. We don't know where he went after he headed off to meet Elizaveta, or the person he thought was Elizaveta.'

He nodded. 'Got it.'

She stocked her backpack with bottled water and biscuits, then returned to her team. She overheard the organisers saying that four groups would be going into town, through the market and into the residential areas. Another would be down on the beach. Willow's group, the smallest, would be tasked with checking the steep path up into the cliffs.

The guy who was supposed to be leading her group was asked to take charge of one of the bigger ones. He turned to Willow.

'You can lead this one, can't you? You know what you're looking for. Really, we just want to rule that area out. It's not the most likely place to find him.'

She nodded, understanding her brief. She turned to her group.

'If everyone is ready, please follow me.'

HALF AN HOUR LATER, she was climbing up a crumbly footpath and looking down at the sea below. Behind her, she heard a couple of Irish tourists speculating about whether Josh might have gone into the water. She looked down at the wild waves. There was no way Josh would have jumped. He had been so happy, having the time of his life.

He could have been drunk, said a little voice in the back of her head. *He could have been wasted and slipped.* But then, why would he have come up here on his own? And why send her a message saying he was okay?

She had handed Josh's phone details over to Radoslav and the police were trying to trace it. She wondered how long it would take. Surely that was the easiest way to find him? Unless someone had him, and they'd disposed of the phone. She tasted stomach acid in her mouth. If they'd disposed of his phone, they might also have disposed of him.

She forced herself to concentrate on the search. It was a

hot, sweaty climb in the heat, but not especially difficult. After the first couple of hours, the other members of the search group gave up. They had combed two separate paths now and covered a lot of ground. She thanked them all for their time, but she was determined to complete the task.

As she and Spence climbed the remaining path, they stumbled upon a small hut nestled in the cliffs. She pushed open the door. Inside was a mattress barely covered by a threadbare blanket.

'Spence! You have to see this.'

Spence poked his head inside the hut. 'Oh, I heard about this place. The locals call it Romeo's palace. It's where the teenagers come to get lucky.'

'Doesn't look like much of a palace to me.'

'Well, no,' he agreed, wrinkling his nose.

The smell wasn't exactly an aphrodisiac.

They continued on their way, leaving behind the unlikely love nest.

'Where do you think Josh is?' she asked as they climbed. 'Tiana is convinced Elizaveta is lying. She could have got her friends to cover for her.'

'But why?'

'I have no idea.'

'What about Kelly? She's always around, always watching everything that goes on.'

'That's true. My mum mentioned her, you know. I think she must know her from back home.'

'Really? Why didn't she say before?'

'I don't know. I didn't think to ask. Hugo has spent the most time with her and he likes her.'

'That's because she makes a fuss of him. You all need to stop fussing around him. He needs to get back on his feet.'

'He's broken his leg!'

'He's milking it.'

'That's not fair.'

'Just saying it as it is.'

Spence fell quiet as they climbed up a steeper part of the cliff. Stones rolled away as she walked, and she had to plant her feet more firmly into the ground.

'We need to keep going', she said, turning around to look at him.

'I'm trying.'

She could see he was flagging. His slowness was starting to annoy her. She needed to get this done. What if Josh was lying injured on the path somewhere?

'I need a break. I'm getting lightheaded.'

Of course, he hadn't eaten. He wasn't much good when he was hungry.

'Have a biscuit. It'll give you some energy.'

'I don't want a biscuit. I need a break.'

'Fine.'

They stopped and drank some water. It felt very calm, just the two of them, like they were the only people left in the world. She leaned her head on his shoulder.

'Have you thought any more about what I asked you? About moving in together?'

'Spence!'

She jerked her head up.

'What?'

'It's hardly the time.'

They both fell silent again. There was an amazing view of the sea below, the rough waves crashing in and out of the rocks.

'I think you already know the answer,' he said. 'I saw your face when I arrived at the airport. I thought you'd be happy to see me, but you never really wanted me to come on this holiday, did you?'

She looked at him, floored. 'You know I love you, Spence. What I can't handle is your moods. I can't commit to spending the rest of my life walking on eggshells.'

The Beach

'I can change.'

'So you say, but people rarely do.'

He let out a puff of air.

'Time to get going again,' she said. She scrambled to her feet and grabbed a stick from the undergrowth, using it to propel herself along.

Spence was right on her heels now.

'Careful, you're tripping me up,' she complained.

She knew he probably wanted to lead, but she wasn't in the mood to accommodate him. Josh was her brother. She had every right to go in front.

The path grew even steeper. She kept on going until a little goat appeared. Its shaggy coat was matted and its horns twisted like branches, but its nimble hooves navigated the path with ease.

'You never said there were going to be goats,' Spence complained.

She thought he was joking. The laughter died on her lips as she turned round and saw he was serious. He acted like the goat was a bear, blocking his path.

'Just push past it. It's fine.'

'That's easy for you to say. Animals like you.'

She wasn't sure if he was actually scared or just tired.

'They sense your fear,' she said, reaching over the goat to give him her hand, but he refused to take it, stubborn as always.

Spence closed his eyes for a moment. He leaned towards her, his voice low and measured. 'You've been stringing me along for months now. One minute you're hot for me, the next cold. Make up your mind, Willow. What do you actually want? Are you going to move in with me, or is it over? I'd rather you just tell me, so I know where I stand.'

She stared at him with incomprehension. 'My brother is missing!'

He acted like he hadn't heard her. 'Because if you don't

want to be with me, I'm not even sure what I'm doing anymore. My life won't be worth living.'

'Oh, don't you dare pull that crap on me!'

She pushed ahead and kept going up the cliff path. It was too hot and she had already drunk most of her water. She just wanted to get to the top, ascertain that Josh was not up there, and get back down. She wasn't sure there was much point now. There wasn't much further to go. He was hardly going to be up there, waiting to congratulate them at the summit.

But there might be evidence of him, she reminded herself. The smallest thing, a button, a shoelace. If there was anything of his up there, she would find it.

A sharp cry pierced her ears. She swung round. Spence was no longer on the path behind her.

Slowly, her gaze dropped to the cliffs below. Her eyes swept between the shoreline, and the waves pummelling the rocks. Then she looked up a bit, and that was when she saw the body on the ledge about ten feet down, limbs twisted at an unnatural angle.

CHAPTER TWENTY-ONE
WILLOW

Willow stared in horror, her eyes straining to make out if it was in fact Spence, because a tiny part of her thought, or even hoped, it might be Josh.

Then the figure twitched and she saw his face more distinctly. He raised one arm up towards her, hands outstretched, giving her a thumbs up.

'Spence!'

He clearly wasn't alright though. The way his body was twisted made her want to puke. She started to climb down towards him, but the earth moved under her feet. She clutched hold of a bush. But she couldn't get a good handhold. She started to tremble. This was no good. What the hell was she doing?

She heard a voice from the footpath above. She looked up and saw a man jogging towards her. He shouted again.

'English?'

'You must not attempt it,' he said, extending his hand to pull her back up to the path. 'This way is very dangerous.'

'I need help! My boyfriend fell.'

She gesticulated wildly. He followed her gaze and when he saw Spence, he let out a loud exclamation before pulling out his phone. She waited as he rang the emergency services. Then he turned to look at her.

'Help is coming. Everything will be okay.'

She cupped her hands over her mouth. 'Help is coming!'

She had no idea if Spence could hear her down there. He lay where he was and didn't make any attempt to move.

'Oh, Spence!' Her heart flooded with emotion.

She shouldn't have pushed him to keep going. He had been hot and angry. She should have given him longer to calm down. Guilt settled heavily in her chest as she made the long, slow walk back down the cliff path.

An ear-splitting roar pierced the sky, and she covered her head with her hands. A helicopter circled above, its blades creating a powerful gust that sent small pebbles skittering across her path. It hovered in the air and her muscles tensed as she watched them carefully secure Spence onto a stretcher and hoist him up. She thought she might be sick as he spun about in the wind, but gradually, they managed to lift his battered body up into the waiting aircraft.

Tears welled in her eyes as she watched the helicopter fly away into the distance. She waved frantically, even though there was no way he could see her from that high up. The sound slowly faded into the background.

'You need a drink,' her rescuer said.

She didn't argue. They stopped at a bar and he ordered in Bulgarian. The bar man pushed a glass in front of her. It smelt strong and alcoholic, exactly what she needed.

'What's your name?' she asked.

'My name is not important. Your brother is the missing Englishman, right?'

She nodded. 'He's been missing a couple of days now. I'm hoping he'll be found today. If not, the police are tracing his phone.'

His eyebrows drew together. 'I wouldn't hold my breath.'

'You don't think they're any good?'

He shook his head. 'They're all either corrupt or incompetent.'

She thought of the kindness Radoslav had shown her. The concern of his colleagues.

'The police are not well paid here, especially at the lower levels. They have to find some way to live. So if they do find Josh, we have to trust they will do the right thing. I wouldn't put it past some of them to try to extract a bribe from whoever took him to keep quiet.'

She swallowed a gulp of her drink. 'You think someone took him?'

'I don't know all the facts of the case, but I'm suspicious that they haven't found any evidence of him. No CCTV footage, no witnesses. Nothing. It's all a bit old school here, which makes it easy to claim a recording is faulty, or the camera didn't record. But the longer it goes on and they find nothing, the more inclined I would be to suspect something is being covered up.'

'What would anyone want with Josh?' She was almost afraid to ask.

He swirled the ice around in his glass. 'Well, it seems to me he's a nice-looking boy. Someone might have taken a shine to him.'

'You think he's been sold into slavery?'

'Maybe, or it could have been a mugging that went wrong and they had to get rid of the evidence.'

She swallowed hard.

Josh was no fighter. He had always been able to talk his way out of anything, but what good were those skills here in Bulgaria, when faced with an opponent who might not even speak English?

'Thanks for the drink. I'd better go and check in with the search.'

'You are welcome.'

She felt his eyes on her as she walked out of the bar and

headed back to the resort.

She wondered how Spence was doing. How bad were his injuries? Would the hospital even know who to call when they got there?

There were a handful of people hanging around the pool, sipping drinks. When Kelly spotted her, she stepped forward.

'Any luck?'

She shook her head. She had heard nothing from Radoslav, and she knew that if Josh had been found, he would have called.

What about her mum? She should be on her way. She didn't know what time her plane would arrive. She desperately hoped there would be some kind of update before she landed. Some kind of good news to give her, because this complete nothing was killing her.

She checked the flight schedule. There was a plane coming in this evening. Maybe she would be on that one. She hoped so. She needed her mum more than anything.

'You should eat something,' Kelly said, nudging her towards the refreshments. There were pastries and bowls of dried fruits set up next to the drinks.

Willow couldn't even look at the food. 'Spence got hurt,' she said tearfully. 'They had to airlift him to hospital.'

'Oh, my!'

Kelly was about to say something more when Radoslav arrived.

'We are pleased with the outcome of the search,' he said. 'We did not find any trace of your brother, but this is good news. Because there is no sign that he has come to any harm.'

Willow nodded, but she dreaded what would come next. She knew the logical move would be to look for him in the sea. But her gut told her that was not where they would find him.

She thought about what that man had told her. Somebody knew where he was. She just had to figure out who.

She turned to see Tiana and Lia walking her way.

'How's it going?' Tiana asked.

Willow shook her head and told them about Spence.

'Oh my god! Have you called his family?'

'He's only got his brother. I don't have his number. I don't even know what hospital they took him to. It's all such a mess.'

'I'll go and have a word with the police,' Tiana offered. 'I'm sure they can help.'

'Thank you.' She glanced at her watch. 'Right. I suppose I'd better go and check on Hugo.'

He was no longer by the pool, so she could only assume he had made it back to the villa. He was getting more mobile, but she still felt guilty for leaving him alone. There was just so much going on right now. So many people to worry about, and she was just one person…

There was a loud splash as a couple of the volunteers stripped down to bathing suits and plunged into the pool. She couldn't blame them for wanting to cool off and have some fun. This was supposed to be a holiday, after all. She looked up and spotted Hugo out on the balcony, watching them from above. She gave him a wave and then her phone started to ring.

Mum!

'Where are you? Are you on your way?'

'I'm still at the airport waiting for a standby flight.'

'There's one this evening.'

'I know, but it's fully booked. I'm hoping someone will miss it.'

'Me too.'

'Don't worry, I'll be there as soon as I can.'

'I know.'

She held the phone tight, wishing she could reach through it and hug her mum.

'Mum, I've got to go, okay? Drop me a text as soon as you know when you're coming.'

'Will do, darling. Stay safe. I love you.'

'I love you too.'

Hugo was still on the balcony when Willow reached the villa. He had a can of coke in front of him, and a newspaper laid on the table. It looked like he'd been doing the crossword.

'How did it go? Any news?'

'Spence fell down the cliff and had to be taken to hospital.'

'You're kidding?'

'No.'

Carefully, she stepped onto the balcony and sat in the other chair. She didn't like it up here. She couldn't help but remember what had happened to Tiana at the beginning of the holiday.

'I'm starting to get really paranoid,' she confessed. 'I feel like we're sitting ducks. Someone is picking us off one by one. I mean, think about it. Josh survived the alcohol poisoning, so they took him.'

'Coincidence doesn't prove correlation,' he said. 'A lot of bad stuff has happened to us, but it might be unrelated.'

'You think?'

'I don't know. I just don't like to jump to conclusions.'

'Me either.'

She looked down at the pool and saw Kelly clearing away the refreshments. Radoslav was standing in front of the kiosk. He spotted her and waved for her to come down.

'Be right back,' she told Hugo.

She stepped down from the balcony and hurried through the house, jogging back down to the pool.

'Ah, Willow. I'm told they have taken Spence to Sofia. He

The Beach

will be in good hands there. They have some of the best surgeons around.'

'How do I contact him?'

'Don't worry. He had his ID in his pocket so they were able to reach his family.'

'But I need to know how he is! No one has told me anything.'

'I'm sorry about that. All I know is that they are operating on his spine. I have left your number with the hospital so they can contact you if needed. I expect he will call you himself once he comes through the surgery.'

'I see. Thank you.'

'And I understand your mother has requested a meeting with my boss as soon as she arrives. You might like to get in on that?'

'Yes, please. Has there been any update on Josh's phone?'

'All I can tell you is that he doesn't appear to be using it.'

'Could the SIM card have been destroyed?'

'That's a possibility, yes. None of Josh's bank cards have been accessed either, which makes it less likely that he's been a victim of a robbery.'

'I see.'

'Now, you'll have to excuse me, I need to get back to the station. I have a lot of paperwork to attend to.'

'Of course. Don't let me keep you.'

All the time she had been talking to Radoslav, Kelly was cleaning down the tables. Once she had finished, she went round wiping them for a second time. The volunteers climbed out of the pool and left. Willow helped Kelly bring in the chairs.

'You don't have to do that,' Kelly said.

'I need to keep busy,' she explained. 'It's all been too much. I feel like I'm losing my mind.'

Kelly wrapped her arms around her. Willow could hear

her heart beating in her chest. It seemed to beat very fast. Da-dum-da-dum-da-dum.

She drew back and finished stacking the chairs. She turned to tell Kelly she was leaving when she noticed the expression on her face. She was talking to herself as she brought in the last chair, but there was something in that expression Willow hadn't noticed before. It was salacious, almost voyeuristic. As if she was getting a kick out of Willow's distress.

CHAPTER TWENTY-TWO
KELLY

I have always believed life is cyclical. I knew it was only a matter of time before it happened again, but fortunately, this time I'm here to put a stop to it.

I was the first on the scene when Tiana fell from her balcony. Because of Pierce, she was saved. It took two of us to get her out of the pool. Willow played her part, but a few more minutes and it would have been too late for both of them.

And I was there when the boys went out drinking that night. I even suggested to young Josh that he should go steady, but would he listen? Of course not. I told Spence that the boys were a mess and he would be best advised to take them home. He seemed reluctant, but somehow, I managed to get through to him.

And after that, it all started to spiral out of control. Pierce's warnings came thick and fast. So many, I could barely keep up with them. Everything was going horribly wrong and there seemed little I could do. I stepped up my rituals, cleaning the tables down over and over. It got to the point where I could barely hold a conversation. It was so hard to listen with Pierce constantly screaming in my ear.

Something is happening. But I am only one person and sometimes it is too much for me to bear. I have reached crisis point. I did my best, but Josh and Willow need their mother. Patsy needs to come out here. She's the only one who can bring them into line.

CHAPTER TWENTY-THREE
WILLOW

Willow's phone started ringing. She grabbed it from her pocket.

'Lia?'

'Come quickly! Tiana's out of control.'

'Where are you?'

'Down the beach, just outside the Golden Hour.'

With a shake of her head, Willow hurried down the path. She spotted Tiana as soon as she set foot on the beach, or rather, she spotted Elizaveta, her long hair tied back in a plait as she tried to wrench something from Tiana's hand.

'Tiana? What's going on?'

Elizaveta glared at her. 'She stole my phone.'

'I just want to get a look at it,' Tiana said, holding it up in the air.

Willow shook her head. 'This isn't the way.'

Tiana glared at her. 'Do you want to find Josh or not? Just hold her off for a minute so I can take a look.'

'You don't even have my password,' Elizaveta said.

'It's already unlocked.'

Willow looked from one to the other. She knew she should help Elizaveta. Tiana had no right to take her phone. But what if Tiana was right? What if she did know something about Josh?

'Just give her a minute,' she begged. 'You'll get your phone back, I promise.'

Elizaveta snarled. 'You're as crazy as your mad dog friend.'

Willow looked over at Lia, pleading with her to do something, but Lia took a step back.

Willow planted herself between Elizaveta and Tiana. Tiana took the phone and moved a little further down the beach, scrolling at lightning speed. It only took her a couple of minutes.

'She doesn't have Josh's number. She didn't send that text. Sorry.'

She held the phone out to Elizaveta, who snatched it back and slipped it into her fake Armani bag.

'The sooner you crazy bitches leave Bulgaria, the better.'

'Sorry,' Willow said again.

As Elizaveta flounced off, Willow's phone beeped.

'It's Mum,' she said, reading the text. 'She's managed to get a flight.'

'That's great,' Tiana said.

Just a few more hours and her mum would be here, and she wouldn't have to feel quite so alone.

THEY HEADED BACK to the villa. Tiana and Lia were planning to return home with Hugo in the morning. They needed to pack. Willow lingered outside, checking her social media accounts to see if anyone had any leads.

She logged onto Facebook and found a community page for Paradise Palms. It was mainly concerned with the buying and selling of items such as baby buggies and second-hand books. Someone had copied and pasted a police update, asking for news of Josh. Willow scanned the comments, but

The Beach

there was nothing new there, just a bunch of women saying how shocking it was that he had gone missing. One of them had linked to another Facebook page. This one was in Bulgarian, but she clicked it anyway.

It was a post from Kelly, appealing for information about Josh. Willow hit the translate button and scanned it carefully. Kelly was not just appealing for information, she was asking that anyone who knew anything came directly to her, rather than the police. Not only that, but she was offering a cash reward.

She glanced over at the kiosk and saw that Kelly was locking up for the night. Kelly seemed to sense her watching.

'I hope they find him soon,' she called. The compassion had returned to her eyes.

'Me too.'

Willow felt guilty for doubting her. Perhaps Kelly didn't trust the police, like the man she had spoken to yesterday. Perhaps she was trying to cut through the corruption and bribery to get to the truth. But if that was the case, why hadn't she mentioned it?

She kept Kelly in her sights as she made her way out of the resort. For all she knew, Kelly was walking towards her car, but as she started down the road that led out of town, it became clear that she was making the journey on foot. Willow's spine tingled, and before she knew what she was doing, she was following her.

She kept her distance. They were the only two people out on the street. There was no one else in sight apart from a few cars driving by. She stayed well back, not wanting to be spotted. How on earth would she explain it if Kelly suddenly turned around and saw her? She kept her head down, ducking behind bushes and trees, feeling like she was playing a spy game, like she had with Josh when they were kids. They used to put on disguises. He inevitably wore a fake moustache and glasses. She swallowed a sob. Where the hell was he?

Kelly turned and headed up a hill. There was a ramshackle cottage a little way ahead, no other buildings in sight. Willow sensed that this was where she was going. The house looked to be in a bad state. The surrounding fence was broken, and there was junk piled up outside, a white Lada parked on the drive. She took out her phone and photographed it. It might come in handy to know what car Kelly drove.

Kelly unlocked the house and disappeared inside. Willow crept across the gravel driveway, cringing at the sound of her steps. It was like walking across cornflakes. Flies buzzed around in the heat as she peered in at the window. Kelly was out of view for about five minutes, then she saw her go into her kitchen. She watched as she opened and closed cupboard doors. How exhausting it must be to cook for yourself after a day working in a kiosk. She took out pasta and tomatoes and sipped a glass of red wine while she chopped and sliced. She spilt a little of the wine down her front, but didn't seem to notice the big red mark bleeding into her pristine white blouse. She sat down at the table and waited for her dinner to cook. It only took about ten minutes or so, and when it was ready, she dished up the food onto two plates.

Who was the other one for?

Kelly sat by herself at the table. Willow waited for another person to appear. Were they already in the house, or was she still expecting someone to arrive?

It occurred to her that she might have prepared a second plate for another meal. Her own mother was a big fan of batch cooking, preparing several portions of whatever she made so that they could just whip it out of the freezer if they didn't have time to cook. Was that all this was? But then she would have put the second portion into a container to be stored in the fridge, whereas she had dished it up onto a plate, and there were now flies buzzing around it.

Kelly ate slowly, twirling the pasta around her fork. She

The Beach

finished her wine and picked up the bottle. She seemed disappointed to find it empty. Then she rose from the table and picked up the other plate. Willow watched with interest as she headed out of the room.

She pressed her nose against the glass, wandering what to do. There was nothing innately suspicious about there being someone else in the house. For all she knew, Kelly had an elderly relative who preferred to eat in their room. And yet her gut told her she was onto something. She needed to get into the house.

Slowly, she tried the door. It opened. If Kelly was keeping Josh in there, wouldn't she keep it locked? Didn't that tell her all she needed to know? She waited a few more minutes. Presently, Kelly came back downstairs, carrying the plate. It still had most of the food on it. Whoever was up there must not be hungry. Kelly left the dishes in the sink and walked away. Willow waited a while, listening intently. She could hear the sound of a TV. This seemed to confirm that Kelly was now settled in the living room.

She reached for the door handle and gave it a gentle twist. It turned easily in her grasp. A surge of adrenaline rushed through her as she pushed it open and slipped inside. She pulled her hood up over her head and moved slowly, tiptoeing into the kitchen. Every creak felt like an explosion in the stillness of the house.

She moved across the kitchen and out into the hallway. The living room door was ajar. Her heart leapt as she spotted Kelly sprawled on the sofa, the remote tucked beneath her arm.

Taking care not to make a sound, she turned and checked the next room. It contained bookcases, a round table and chairs. She kept moving towards the other side of the house, where she found the stairs. She paused and listened. Not a sound came from the upstairs bedrooms, but she could still hear the TV chattering away to itself.

The stairs creaked as she stepped on them. She paused, waiting to see if the noise would alert Kelly. When nothing happened, she kept going, putting one foot in front of the other until she reached the first floor.

There were three doors. She tried the first one and found the bathroom. It was decorated with pictures of angels: blond haired cherubs, all round and cuddly. The window sill was crammed with various face creams and serums, tubes of make up and deodorant. The bath had a towel flung over the side of it, and in the little pot, there was one single toothbrush. Did this mean Kelly lived alone after all? What about the second plate of food? Could she have a dog, perhaps? But no dog worth its salt would have left the plate unfinished. Besides, it would have started barking the moment Willow entered the house.

She stopped and listened. She thought she heard a noise from downstairs. The sound of a door creaking. The opening and closing of a cupboard. Perhaps Kelly had gone to get herself a drink. As quietly as she could, she tiptoed towards the next room. She opened it softly and saw a neat double bed made-up with an old-fashioned quilt. There was a dressing table covered with perfumes and a load of those VivaLux products Tiana sold. There was a strong smell of perfume throughout the house, and another, funkier odour that she couldn't identify.

She let herself out. There was only one door left. She reached for the handle. It turned easily, and she peered inside. She was immediately hit by the smell. It was rotten and cloying. She scanned the room. There was a bunk bed, made up with colourful duvets, a He-Man one on the top, Spiderman on the bottom. The top bunk appeared to be empty, but the bottom one was occupied. The figure was completely hidden under the duvet.

CHAPTER TWENTY-FOUR
WILLOW

She should have left. She had no way of knowing this person had anything to do with Josh, and yet her gut told her that she needed to check. She didn't know what she was going to do, what she was going to say if it was anyone other than her brother. They would probably scream, call the police. Who knew, but she couldn't bear it. She had to know.

She tiptoed across the room, step by step, her heart in her mouth. Her hand shook as she reached out and slowly peeled back a corner of the duvet.

The stench of death hit her like a physical force. A putrid mix of mustiness and decay that made her gag. She pulled the duvet back further, fear pounding in her chest.

She stifled a scream as she took in what she was looking at. Her heart hammered and she shook all over. She stuffed her fist into her mouth, biting down in her anguish. No one should ever have to see such an abomination.

She was looking at skin mottled with rot and covered with a layer of grime. Where there should have been hair, there was only a bare skull, with hollowed eye sockets staring back at her. She breathed into her fist, unable to stop the strangled sound that escaped her lips.

A fly landed on the decaying body, its wings buzzing relentlessly against the sunken cheekbones. She forced herself to breathe, taking in the deep hollows and jagged edges of the corpse. One skeletal hand poked out from under the blanket. The fingers were bony and pointy, with long, razor sharp nails. She dropped the duvet and backed away. Footsteps echoed on the stairs and she froze in place, fear coursing through her veins.

Frantically, she looked around for somewhere to hide. The only place she could think of was the top bunk. There was no ladder to reach it. She put one foot on the bottom bunk and hoisted herself up onto the thin mattress, hoping she hadn't dislodged the bones below. She laid low and pulled the covers over her head, and tried to muffle the sound of her breathing as the footsteps grew closer. The rotting smell made her nose tingle, but she resisted the urge to sneeze, staying perfectly still as Kelly entered the room.

The floor creaked and her heart pounded in her ears. Kelly approached the bed, speaking softly, and sang a lullaby. Then she fell silent, and Willow wondered if she had been discovered. She risked a peek and saw that Kelly was sitting with her head bowed. Her lips moved slightly, whilst holding one skeletal hand in her own.

She strained to hear the words she was speaking. They reminded her of one of Spence's poems:

The winds raged,
Whipping through the waves,
With a ferocity that threatened to tear us asunder,
I stared death in the eye, but it did not break me.
Because my love for you,

The Beach

> Is woven from the deepest pain.
> My heart beats for two.
> Together we are invincible
> In this life and the next.
> God help anyone who would tear us apart.
> God help us all.

WHAT WAS THIS, some kind of prayer?

All was still for a moment, and Willow had the weirdest feeling, like Kelly was sitting there, waiting for her to reveal herself. She sat in silence for at least ten minutes. It felt like longer. Willow shut her eyes and focused on the rhythmic rise and fall of her breathing, and she wondered if Kelly could hear the pounding of her heart. The creaks and groans of the old house seemed amplified. Every bang of the window shutters echoed through the room.

Kelly stood abruptly, as if she had just snapped out of a trance. She murmured something to the body in the bed, then walked haltingly to the door. There was a stiffness to her gait now. With a creaking sound, she disappeared into the adjacent bedroom, closing the door with a soft click.

Willow's eyes fluttered open and she let out a deep breath.

Where the hell are you, Josh?

She pulled her phone from her pocket and brought up Radoslav's number. She didn't dare call him. Kelly might hear. Instead, she fired out a text:

Found a dead body at Kelly's house. It can't be Josh. It looks much older.

She paused, trying to remember the address. She gave directions as best she could and clicked send.

Slowly, she lowered herself down from the top bunk, her arms shaking with exhaustion. The rusty metal frame groaned under her weight as her feet hit the cold surface. She held onto the railing for support, swinging slightly as she struggled to find her balance.

A wave of revulsion washed over her as her foot grazed against the bony fingers of the skeleton. She imagined its hand reaching out to grab her ankle, causing her to stumble and lose control. She stopped still, remaining motionless as she strained to see if Kelly would come to investigate, but all was still.

She crept past Kelly's bedroom and stole quietly down the stairs. Shadows danced in the dim light as she made her way through the house, darting between the furniture, towards the kitchen. She reached the door and tried the handle. She rattled it, but it wouldn't open. The door was stuck.

Not just stuck. Locked.

She looked around, scanning the countertops. With a plunging sensation, she realised Kelly might have the key on her person. Desperately, she tried the drawers, but it was nowhere to be seen. Then she caught sight of a hook beside the cooker. There was a metal key hanging there. She took it down and tried it in the door. It was a bit stiff, but it worked. Her fingers reached for the handle just as her phone started to ring.

Shit!

She grabbed it from her pocket and fumbled for the off switch, but it was too late. A shadow fell over her.

'Hey you! What the hell do you think you're doing?'

Willow froze. She didn't dare look round. It was possible Kelly hadn't seen her face, and she still had her hood up, hiding her giveaway red hair. She pressed down on the door handle and burst out into the fresh air. Crickets chirped as she dashed down the path without looking back. Kelly wouldn't be able to catch her now, not if she kept to the shadow of the trees. But she might have recognised her. She waited until she was sure she had lost her, then she checked to see who had called. It was her mum. She had arrived at the airport.

She took a ragged breath and kept walking, keeping her head down as she headed back down the silent road towards Paradise Palms.

CHAPTER TWENTY-FIVE
KELLY

My stomach churns as Willow runs out of my house. She's seen you, Pierce. What is she going to do? What are we going to do? I can't let her interfere. I can't lose you. Not after so many years.

My mind drifts back to that terrible time ten years ago. Your body was released to me so that I could transport you back to England. I drove you to the docks myself in a hire van and waited for the boat that was going to take you home. But the boat was late, and the longer we waited, the more certain I became that I couldn't let go of you.

'Take me home Mum', you whispered.

'I'm trying.'

'Not back to England, to the holiday house.'

The house I was staying in belonged to an elderly couple who usually rented to tourists. They'd taken pity on me, after reading about us in the papers, and said I could stay as long as I needed.

I saw a boat on the horizon, and realised with a jolt that it was your boat coming to take you away. Before I knew what I was doing, I was turning the van around and driving back to the house.

It wasn't easy getting you inside. Don't even get me started on the stairs. And I had to wait until nightfall, because I was worried about the nosey neighbours. But somehow, I got you inside, and eventually I got you up the stairs and tucked you into bed. I bandaged you up like a mummy in those early days, but I can't have done it right, because your body disintegrated in spite of my efforts.

You're still in there, though. Nothing brings me greater comfort than wrapping my arms around you and tucking you in every night. I have made myself a part of this community. People like and respect me, but I keep my distance from all of them, because no one must ever know the truth about us. And I don't think anyone has ever suspected. Not until now.

CHAPTER TWENTY-SIX
PATSY

Burgas airport was a bustling hub of activity as Patsy manoeuvred her suitcase through the crowd. The smell of fried food and the constant chatter in different languages assaulted her senses. She hadn't been able to eat on the plane, so now she grabbed a flaky pistachio roll on her way to the taxi rank.

She joined the queue, biting her tongue as others talked and laughed with excitement about their holidays. She wondered how many of these people were heading to Paradise Palms.

When she reached the front of the queue, the taxi driver helped her with her suitcase, effortlessly lifting it into the boot while she gratefully sank into the back seat. She wanted to sleep, but he kept talking to her, pointing out sites of interest as they drove through the sprawling city.

It wasn't yet dark, so she had a chance to take in the buildings and lakes. What a shame to be visiting this lovely place in such circumstances.

'Are you here for the week?' he asked.

She drew a breath. When she told him the true purpose of her visit, he looked sad.

"You should call the TV station and ask them to put his picture up on the news.'

'I will be meeting with the police when I get there. I'll suggest it to them.'

They both fell silent until they arrived at Paradise Palms. She gazed up in awe at the tall, swaying palm trees. The golden sand glittered in the moonlight. She took in the lush greenery and dark blue water, but her eyes scanned the horizon, searching desperately for any sign of Josh. She half expected him to jump out from behind a tree, or emerged bedraggled from the sea, as if all this time, he had just been waiting for her to arrive.

In contrast to the airport, the resort seemed quiet, desolate even. The moment the taxi pulled away, an overwhelming sense of emptiness washed over her. She had thought she would sense his presence here. She had thought she would feel instantly that he was alive. But all she felt was emptiness and grief.

A few people lingered outside the bars. Their voices carried in the night air, blending together in a rapid stream of Bulgarian. They spoke so fast, she couldn't tell when one word ended and another began.

The pool area was deserted, the sun loungers stacked up against the fence. She scanned the perimeter and spotted Kelly's kiosk. She had been hoping to speak to her, but of course, it was too late for that. She was closed for the day.

Disappointed, she pulled out a crumpled bit of paper and checked the address she had been given for the villa. The kids were originally supposed to vacate on Sunday, but Willow had got permission to stay on a few more days. She followed Willow's instructions, her suitcase rattling behind her as she walked the last few yards and knocked on the door.

'Come in', a voice called. It sounded like Hugo. She pushed open the door and saw him with his leg propped up on a stack of cushions.

'What the hell happened to you?'

'Kitesurfing accident.'

'Oh, you poor boy!'

Her arms instinctively reached out for him, her embrace filled with the same warmth and love she longed to give her own son. The tightness in her chest was unbearable as she pulled away. Her eyes scanned the corridor for Willow.

Tiana and Lia emerged from one of the adjourning rooms.

'Mrs Spicer!' They said in unison.

She smiled sadly. 'Hello girls. Where's Willow?'

They looked at each other uncertainly.

'I think she went out,' Tiana said.

'Out where?'

'Not sure. I think she's looking for Josh again.'

Patsy frowned. 'Did Spence go with her?'

'You haven't heard?'

'Heard what?'

'Spence fell down a cliff.'

Patsy's hand went to her heart. 'Oh my goodness! Was he seriously hurt?'

All three teenagers looked blank, and she fought the urge to throttle them.

'It only happened this afternoon. He was taken to Sofia by helicopter. The last we heard, he's in surgery.'

She sat down heavily. 'So let's get this straight. Two of you are injured. Josh is missing, and Willow's out on her own?'

'I'm sure she'll be back soon,' Lia said softly. 'Can I get you a cup of tea, Mrs Spicer?'

She forced herself to smile.

'It's Patsy, and yes please. A cup of tea would be very welcome.'

She dialled Willow's number. 'She's not answering?'

'The phone coverage is a bit patchy,' Hugo said.

'Right.'

She tucked her phone back in her pocket. She had known both the girls since they were tiny, but she had only known Hugo a couple of years. She recalled him cracking jokes on sports day, rather than taking part. Josh's event had always been the long jump. He wasn't as tall as some of the others, but he always gave it his all. She remembered the look of pride on his face when he was awarded his little silver medal. Then Willow had won the gold in the 100m and he had slipped it into his pocket, as if his sister's achievement had cancelled out his own. He had always defined his achievements in relation to Willow's. That was how close they were.

She sipped the hot tea Lia brewed for her and felt its comforting warmth spread through her body, reviving her tired muscles. She rubbed her mouth. She had been clenching her jaw again, she realised.

'How did Josh seem the last time you spoke to him?' she asked. 'Did he seem worried at all?'

Hugo shook his head. 'He seemed completely normal. He said he had had a text from Elizaveta, inviting him to play tennis, and he would bring me pizza on his way back, but he never did.'

Gathering up her strength, she set down her cup and pushed herself up from the chair. Her next move was to walk down to the police station. She had already located it on the map. She wanted to see how seriously they were taking Josh's disappearance. She wondered if the story had hit the papers back at home yet. She had contacted a couple of journalists while she was at the airport. They had both seemed interested and concerned for him. She just hoped he didn't get bumped for a bigger story. There had been something about those VivaLux beauty products in the morning papers. The business had unexpectedly collapsed, causing hundreds of consultants to lose all the money they had invested.

. . .

Walking through the town, she felt as if all eyes were on her. There were people gathering outside the bars, or queueing for the night club. Some of them looked rather old to be going clubbing, but who was she to judge?

She got the feeling everyone knew who she was. They somehow sensed it, that she must be the mother of the missing boy. The bouncers on the door of the night club shifted their eyes as if they were afraid she was going to come over and lecture them for not watching out for her son.

It was a small community. She had been happy about that. This place was not so large that people went unnoticed. So how was it there had been no sightings of Josh from the moment he went missing? Looking around now, she couldn't believe no one had seen him. He was so handsome, her boy. People had always noticed him. Girls had always stared. There was no way that nobody knew what had happened to him. No way in hell.

The police station was quiet when she arrived, the only sound coming from the soft hum of the florescent lights. She fidgeted with her hands as she approached the front desk. As soon as she opened her mouth, the policeman on duty looked up.

'You must be Josh's mother?'

'Yes… Patsy.'

'You look just like your daughter.'

'Thank you.'

She was shown to a small waiting area, where she sat in an uncomfortable metal chair. After a few minutes, a tall man appeared. He wore a creased linen suit, his thick black hair swept back from his forehead with a strong gel.

'Mrs Spicer? I'm Detective Grigoryev. Come on through.'

He led her into a small room with a big table in the middle. He gestured towards a chair and she sat down. A young woman brought her a cup of strong black coffee. She accepted it gratefully and took a sip. It was full of sugar. She set it to one side while Grigoryev talked her through the investigation.

'We've had search teams everywhere that we can think of and I'm afraid it's now time to start exploring the water,' he said.

Patsy swallowed. Dread settled in her stomach.

'My son is not in the water. I would know. I would feel it.'

He nodded gravely. 'All the same, we have to rule it out. We've got experts arriving in the morning to help pinpoint where he might be.'

'I'm telling you, he's not in the water.'

'Listen, if you want us to find Josh, you have to let us do our job. And that means looking everywhere, following every lead we can. Do you understand?'

She nodded, feeling as though her mind and body were drifting away from each other. She tried to focus on the conversation, but the dizziness only grew stronger, until she had to get some air.

She stumbled outside, her mind spinning like a wheel. She crouched down, with her head between her knees. As she waited for the nausea to pass, she saw a policeman hurry past.

'Hello? Yes, it's Radoslav. Sorry to be calling so late, but I need to come and speak to you about something. You're still up? That's great. It won't take long, I promise.'

She watched as he mounted a bicycle and pedalled furiously away.

ONCE SHE WAS FEELING a little better, she started walking back towards the resort. The leaves rustled in the breeze, sending shivers down her spine. But nothing could compare to the fear that consumed her as she pictured Josh in the depths of the sea. No, it couldn't be true. She gazed up at the glimmering stars, feeling small and helpless in the vastness of the night sky.

Suddenly, she saw someone walking towards her on the road. Her heart raced. She knew that walk. They ran into each other's arms, tears mingling as they held each other tightly.

'Mum! Thank god! You're never going to…'

A loud melody pierced the silent street.

Willow fished in her pocket for her phone and pressed it to her ear.

'Hello?'

She listened briefly, barely speaking a word, before hanging up. Her face was pale in the moonlight.

'What is it?'

She was trembling all over.

'It's…it's Spence. His brother says it's serious. I have to get there straight away. I'll have to fly to Sofia.'

CHAPTER TWENTY-SEVEN
PATSY

They raced back to the villa. Patsy searched for available flights while Willow darted about, grabbing her passport, toothbrush, and other essentials. She managed to book a flight, but they didn't know where she was going to stay.

'Spence's brother is there already,' Willow said as they waited for the taxi. 'We'll sort it all out when I get there. I'm not sure how long…' she stared down at her hands.

Poor Willow. This was all unbelievable.

'Taxi's here!' Tiana yelled.

Patsy hugged her daughter. She didn't want to let her go. She hated the thought of her flying off to a strange city, all on her own. And poor, poor Spence. She couldn't believe this was happening. She prayed to God that Willow's arrival would spurn his recovery.

After Willow left, Patsy stayed at the villa with the others. Tiana, Lia, and Hugo all sat around the living room, their suitcases piled up in the middle.

'There's pizza if you want some,' Lia said.

Patsy shook her head. Her stomach churned, but she didn't feel like eating.

'We should really go to sleep.' Tiana said. 'We've got an early start in the morning.'

Patsy nodded. She should sleep too, and yet nobody headed to bed. They were all too awake, too full of adrenaline. The young people hung around, drinking some weird tasting blackcurrant schnaps the previous tenants had left behind.

'Talk me through it,' she said, after a lengthy pause. 'When was the last time anybody actually saw Josh?'

Tiana thought back. 'I saw him that morning, but he was gone when we got back from Sozapol.'

Hugo nodded. 'He left not long after you. Like, about ten minutes later.'

'This Elizaveta. What does she look like?'

'She's pretty in a really obvious way,' Tiana said, sourly. 'She has really long dark hair, right down to her waist.'

'Small breasts,' Hugo said.

'Tall? Short?'

They all looked at each other.

'Average, I suppose,' Tiana said.

'We told the police about her,' Lia said. 'They'll have questioned her, won't they?'

'I bloody hope so,' Patsy said. She made a note to check next time she spoke to Detective Grigoryev.

She checked her phone. There were no messages from Willow yet. She hoped she had made it to the airport in time.

As Tiana and Lia said goodnight and headed to their own beds, Patsy followed suit. Since Hugo had decided he was more comfortable in the living room, she went into the boy's bedroom and laid down on Josh's bed. The familiar scent of his deodorant clung to the sheets. As she snuggled into the pillows, she felt a lump underneath. Curious, she reached under and pulled out a worn teddy bear. It was Reggie. She couldn't believe he had brought him on holiday.

'Oh, Josh!'

She held the bear close, his soft fur absorbing the steady stream of tears cascading down her face. Josh used to hold Reggie in the same way whenever he was upset. She tried to calm herself enough to fall asleep, but her throat was dry from crying, so she got up in search of water.

She tiptoed out into the corridor, not wanting to wake the others. The dim light from the moon revealed Hugo's silhouette in the kitchen, his back turned to her. He gazed out the window, into the darkness, apparently lost in thought. She hesitated, not wanting to interrupt. As he moved around the room, she noticed he wasn't using his crutches. In fact, he seemed to be walking with ease. A flicker of confusion crossed her mind before she retreated, as silently as she knew how.

CHAPTER TWENTY-EIGHT
WILLOW

Willow's taxi screeched to a halt in front of the hospital, and she stumbled out, her heart racing. It wasn't hard to pick out Spence's brother, Tom. He had the same lanky build and pensive eyes. He had never been much of a hugger, but now he crushed her into his arms.

'I'm so glad you're here.'

She pulled back. 'I still don't understand what happened. The last I heard he was going into surgery?'

'The doctors were initially concerned about a spinal injury. They were preparing him for an operation but…'

He stopped, his face crumpled with pain, before he could continue.

'They said he had a bleed on the brain. There is damage to his heart too. It's all too much for his body to take. The doctor told me quite bluntly that they don't expect him to make it through the night.'

His words were like a punch in the gut. She couldn't believe that after everything she had been through, she was going to lose him. She and Spence had so much unfinished business.

The Beach

'He keeps asking for you. He's holding on, waiting for you to get here.'

Tears filled Willow's eyes as they reached Spence's room. She didn't want to go in. If he was holding on for her, did that mean he was going to give up as soon as he saw her? She tried to blank out their last furious conversation.

'Willow?'

She swallowed hard. She didn't want to say goodbye, but she also couldn't bear the thought of him passing without seeing him one last time.

Taking a deep breath, she pushed open the door and stepped inside. There was a nurse in the corner, quietly monitoring his progress. She took a step towards the bed. Spence lay hooked up to machines and monitors, a big bandage wrapped around his head. His eyes were closed, but as she entered, a weak smile formed on his lips.

'I knew… you'd come.'

With tears streaming down her face, she kissed him gently, then sat down and reached for his hand.

'I love you so much,' she whispered.

She waited, but he didn't reply.

'Are you in pain?' she asked, looking at the drip.

His eyes fluttered open and flicked from one side to the other, as though he were trying to communicate.

The nurse turned and met her gaze, her eyes filled with understanding. 'Don't worry, he should be comfortable.'

Willow nodded and kept her attention on Spence.

'I'm here now. You can relax.'

'Josh?'

Her throat tightened and she forced herself to breathe normally. She wished she had some news for him. Something to ease his pain.

'Josh is… Josh is fine. Absolutely fine.'

She forced her lips into a bright smile and held back the

tears that threatened to fall. When Spence finally looked up at her, that was the last thing he saw.

With a final exhale, he closed his eyes again and drifted away. All at once, the room felt colder, the air more heavy. She became aware of the nurse shifting in her seat, and Tom inching into the room from the doorway. No one said a word, but they all knew what was happening. She stayed by his side for as long as she was allowed, and waited for his spirit to leave his body.

CHAPTER TWENTY-NINE
KELLY

I am still reeling from the break in at my house, when my peace is shattered once again.

I am not surprised to receive a message from Radoslav. I've seen him talking to Willow on multiple occasions. It makes sense that she would go running to him.

The last thing I feel like is company, but I paste a smile onto my lips as I open the door.

'Apologies for the lateness of the hour…'

'Not a problem. I was just going to have some tea and cake. Would you care to join me?'

He's a little rough around the edges, this policeman, but still too polite to refuse me.

'Thank you. You're most kind.'

There is a skittishness to him as he manoeuvrers himself into my kitchen. I watch him hesitate as he seems to consider taking off his shoes, then decides against it.

We sip tea, and I read regret in his features. He doesn't want to be here. In fact, he wishes he was almost anywhere else. So why did he come? Out of a sense of…what, duty? I almost laugh out loud at the thought.

I use the opportunity to quiz him about the investigation

into Josh's disappearance. He answers cagily, knowing he shouldn't reveal too much, but a little gossip is required.

'There's been no sighting, not here or in any of the surrounding towns. We're moving the search wider, checking the water, but also moving out further to other towns and villages in case he went off exploring. Frankly, it doesn't look good. If he had simply wandered off, someone would have seen him.'

'So you think he's come to harm?'

'It's looking increasingly likely, isn't it?'

He meets my eye briefly, as if trying to assess my own depth of knowledge. Then he makes a clumsy attempt at guessing my mental state.

'I'm so lacking in sleep, I'm not even sure what day it is…'

'It's Saturday,' I tell him.

'That's right. I wasn't even supposed to be working. I have the next three days off, but I'm sure I'll go in anyway. The team will need me, with so much to do.'

I nod and cut a slice of the lemon cake I made earlier. 'More cake?'

'You are good to me, but no thank you. I've had quite enough. Actually, would it be alright if I use your bathroom?'

'Be my guest. It's right at the top of the stairs.'

He traipses dirt up my stairs and I sit calmly, listening to his movements. Because I know it is not the bathroom he is looking for. I glance down at the items I lifted from his pockets: his phone and his radio. The phone is still unlocked, so I take the opportunity to message Willow, advising her to remain quiet about what she has told me. Telling her the investigation is still ongoing.

Then I head upstairs to Pierce's room, unsurprised but disappointed nonetheless to see Radoslav stooped over my son. He hears me come in and turns, palms up.

'You can't keep him here. This isn't sanitary.'

I narrow my eyes. 'You knew him, didn't you? You must

have done. You're from here. You will have seen him when he came here on holiday. You're about the same age.'

He blinks rapidly.

'No, I never met him. But listen, I can help you. I can make the arrangements. We can do it discretely. No one needs to know.'

'Your mother had a job cleaning the villas. You used to help her, didn't you? Why did you never say anything? In all the time I've known you.'

'Sorry, you've lost me.'

I step closer. 'The police said it was an accident, but the coroner wasn't so sure. He said Pierce might have been pushed. Only, the police let it slide. The funny thing is, it was just a few months later that you joined up, isn't that right? You made a mistake, didn't you? It was just a stupid childish prank. You were filled with remorse, so you decided the best thing to do would be to serve the public. That's why you've been so desperate to find this English boy. So you can finally atone for your crime. Well, I have news for you. It doesn't work like that.'

He staggers backward. The drugs I put in his tea were potent, and he is already losing the use of his legs.

I wait for him to confess, but his words are increasingly incoherent, as if his mouth is filled with worms. He is sensing it too. I can see it in the widening of his pupils and the way he grips the wall for support. His free hand goes to his pocket and comes up empty. He looks at me in horror. His mouth is going like a yo-yo.

'What have you done?' his words are barely audible.

'What have you done?' I echo.

'My...boss will realise I'm missing. People will come looking for me.'

'Got a high opinion of yourself, haven't you? I don't think your boss particularly rates you. And even if he did, he couldn't find a flea on a street dog. It'll be weeks before anyone's seriously bothered about you, and by then, all trace of you will be gone.'

'No! Please, I'm begging you!'

'Then tell me the truth. How did Pierce really die?'

Radoslav struggles against his own body. I watch as he falls clumsily to the floor and lies there, drool pooling on the carpet. I place my foot on his neck. He's so weak, he can't even fight me off.

'Talk! And no bullshit. I want the honest, ugly truth.'

A hissing sound escapes his lips and I realise I'm pressing a bit too hard. I release the tension and he gasps for air.

'All right, I'll tell you!'

I lean against the doorjamb. 'I'm listening.'

'He was up here with his mates, having a party. They were all getting high, doing whatever they wanted, as if they thought there were no consequences. One night, I saw him getting it on with another guy, right up on the balcony where anyone could walk by. It made me so angry, that complete lack of respect. There were families staying at the resort at that time, and locals working here. But your son and his friends didn't give a damn. I knew where my mother kept the keys, so I went back the following morning. I just wanted to teach him a lesson, so when I saw him leaning over the balcony, I pushed him into the pool. It was only supposed to be a warning. I never imagined he was going to drown. If I had known that, I never would have done it. I promise you, I'm no murderer. Just an angry, foolish young man.'

I close my eyes. His words are so painful to hear, and yet they have a ring of truth about them.

'Thank you for finally being honest with me.'

I wrap my arms around him and hold him tight while he takes his last breath.

CHAPTER THIRTY
PATSY

Patsy sat on Josh's bed, uncertain what to do. She was till thirsty. She wouldn't be able to sleep until she had drunk some water. But she felt less certain of herself. She had always thought Hugo was a decent boy. A bit loud and obnoxious, but decent all the same. But now she wasn't so sure. Either he had experienced a miraculous recovery, or he had been lying about his leg the whole time. Deliberately deceiving everyone, but for what possible end?

Her mind whirled, turning over the various possibilities. If Hugo's leg wasn't injured, then that meant no one had a clue what he had been up to for all those hours when the others had been out of the house. That day, Willow had visited Sozopol, for example. Or when Josh was supposedly off playing tennis. He could have been up to anything, and no one would have been any the wiser.

She waited for as long as she could bear before walking back out into the corridor. By then, Hugo had positioned himself back on the sofa. He appeared to be asleep. She headed into the kitchen without turning the light on. She could just make out the cupboard where the glasses were kept. She took one down, then pulled a bottle of mineral water from the fridge. She filled her glass and took a long drink, feeling relief as the water slid down her throat.

As she quenched her first, a growing sense of unease washed over her. She became aware of someone behind her, watching her every move.

She spun around, heart hammering, and saw Hugo leaning on his crutches, a strange smile playing on his lips.

'I thought it was you,' he said.

It wasn't his usual cheeky grin; this one had more depth and maturity. He was looking at her like he had just noticed she was a woman.

She was suddenly aware that she was dressed in little more than a long T-shirt. She felt his eyes trail her body, and her stomach churned.

'This must be so hard for you.' If he was intending to sound sympathetic, he failed.

His eyes lingered just a little too long on her thighs.

She set down her drink on the counter and reached instead for the bottle opener. It had a nice, jagged edge.

'You know what I think?' he said suddenly.

She clutched the bottle opener a little tighter. 'What?'

'Maybe that girl, Elizaveta, has a relative who didn't like him.'

'Everyone likes Josh.'

She said it automatically, instinctively.

His jaw clenched tightly. 'Not everyone.'

She gulped air involuntarily.

Was Hugo jealous of Josh? He wasn't a wallflower, but he didn't have Josh's good looks.

'Well, it's a thought,' she said lightly.

Abruptly, she made for the door, ducking under his arm in one smooth movement.

She was about to scuttle back to her room when something occurred to her.

The Beach

'Did you have any trouble with your insurance company?' she asked.

'What?'

'Because of your leg? Only, my friend Misha broke her leg when she was skiing in Switzerland one year, and the insurance company wouldn't allow her to fly back.'

He stared at her for a moment, then smiled. 'Well, I won't tell them if you don't.'

She walked back to her room. Well, technically, it was Hugo's room too. But he shouldn't follow, not if he still expected her to believe he was injured.

She shunted her suitcase across the room to block the door and climbed back into Josh's bed, still clutching the bottle opener in her right hand. With her left, she sought out Reggie and laid him on her chest, listening as Hugo rattled around the living room. What was he doing when he was supposed to be getting up in a few hours?

She lay awake, listening. It sounded as though Hugo couldn't sleep either. She heard a rumble of laughter and realised he was watching TV. She tried to stay awake, but her exhausted body had other plans.

In her dream, she wandered barefoot along the shoreline, squinting against the bright sun. Josh was swimming. His sun-kissed skin glistened as he dived in and out of the crystal clear water like a dolphin. He dived and surfaced, the length of time drawing out longer with each dive. She waited anxiously until he popped up to the surface again, emerging with a handful of shimmering pearls.

'Do you like them?' he asked eagerly. 'I'll get you some more!'

'No, Josh! Wait!'

He gave her a mischievous look and then he was gone, back into the sea. She chased after him, wading into the water, but she couldn't find him. She cupped her hands around her mouth.

'Josh, stop! I just want you back!'

She waited. There was an eerie stillness and when she looked down, she realised the water had changed from clear to black.

She opened her eyes and blinked. He wasn't dead. He was still out there somewhere. He had to be.

She pulled the suitcase away from the door and peered into the corridor. The pile of suitcases was gone. The girl's bedroom was wide open and she saw that Hugo's things were gone, too. They must have already left for the airport.

She headed into the kitchen and opened the fridge. She pulled out bacon and eggs and began to cook herself a full English when a text came through from Willow:

S<small>PENCE IS DEAD</small>.

T<small>HAT WAS ALL IT SAID</small>. She dropped the spoon she was holding and leaned against the table, her body unable to endure any more pain.

CHAPTER THIRTY-ONE
WILLOW

Willow's eyes stung from the harsh fluorescent lights as she and Tom walked out of the hospital and crossed the road to the small 24-hour cafe. Sofia was alive with people having fun, partying, and here they were, on one of the bleakest days of her life.

Her heart felt physically heavy, as though it might fall out of her chest. Her grief for Spence battled for space with her increasing anxiety over Josh. She didn't know how much more she could take.

Whilst they drank their coffee, she texted her mum to let her know what had happened. Tom was planning to stay on and take care of all the arrangements to bring Spence home. Willow felt like she was in the middle of an invisible tug of war. Tom looked so sad. He had raised Spence since he was seven because both of their parents had been incapable and now, here he was all alone.

'I didn't want him to go,' he confessed. 'I hated the idea of him being out here, partying all night long, with no one to take care of him. But there was no point arguing about it. You know Spence.'

'I wish he hadn't come,' she said. 'I can't believe he won't be waiting for me when I get home.'

'He loved you so much.'

'I loved him too.'

'He was always in so much of a hurry to grow up. He wanted to get married and have a big family, to make up for what he never had.'

'He never told me that,' she confessed. It didn't entirely surprise her. He had always been so serious, so intense. But they'd barely talked about children, except the odd comment in passing. She hadn't known that was his game plan.

Tom took her hand across the table. 'He talked about you so much. If you cared for him half as much as he cared for you, you must be in agony right now.'

'I am,' she said, removing her hand to wipe away a tear. Now was not the time to tell him they had been close to breaking up. There would probably never be a right time for that.

'Then stay. Help me sort out all the legal stuff. We need to get his ashes back to England and arrange his funeral. I feel like you should be a part of that.'

'I…I'm sorry. My brother is still missing. I have to go back to Paradise Palms.'

He dropped his head. 'Yes. Yes, of course. Do what you have to do.'

He put his hand in his pocket and brought out a small red notebook. She recognised it instantly.

'They found it in his pocket. I think he would want you to have it.'

'Thank you.' She clutched it to her heart. 'I will treasure it always.'

She looked out the window at all the happy people enjoying their night out. She had watched enough TV to know that the chances of finding Josh alive got lower with every passing day. There was no time to lose. She took out her phone and booked herself on the first plane back to Burgas in the morning.

She didn't open Spence's notebook until she was on the plane. Spence had filled every space with poetry and drawings. One or two were quite explicit. She hoped Tom hadn't looked too closely. They were clearly of her. She turned the pages, reading anything that caught her eye. So many poems. Some, Spence had recited for her. Others were new. She stopped on the last page. This poem had a strange title:

The Wolfman

He hugs you,
Like a snake's embrace
Words like honey,
Leave a bitter taste.
Dressed to impress
But he's no lamb
The truth is plain to see,
Even for an idiot like me.
He likes to share,
His words are kind,
But deep inside,
There's nothing there.
So watch your back,
Or he'll attack,
He's not your friend,
It's just pretend.

She turned the page and found a drawing of a wolf with a sinister smile. At its feet was what looked like a slaughtered lamb, blood dripping from its neck. She looked a little closer. It was wearing a tartan scarf.

THE FIRST STREAKS of pink and orange painted the sky as she stepped off the plane at Burgas airport. The shuttle bus was packed with crying infants and weary parents. They all headed for the taxi rank while she walked past to the bus stop to catch the bus back to Paradise Palms.

The bus arrived and she slumped down in an empty seat, resting her head against the window. The closer they got to Paradise Palms, the stronger she felt Josh's presence. She didn't see herself as a spiritual person, and yet the feeling was overpowering. Josh was near. She was certain of it.

She had had a text from Radoslav:

The body belongs to Kelly's deceased son, Pierce, and there does not appear to be any connection to Josh. I strongly advise you to keep what you found to yourself, in order to avoid criminal charges being brought against you for entering her home. Bulgarian law has harsh penalties against home invasions.

She blinked, surprised the police had investigated so quickly. Still, it was good to know what was happening. She still had questions, but perhaps she could bring those up with him later.

The bus dropped her off at the harbour. She was just in time to see the police divers board two boats and set off in their search for Josh. She watched until they were out of sight, then she walked along the pier, looking for somewhere to get coffee. Just as she spotted a little van, her phone started to ring. She didn't recognise the number.

'Hello?'

'Willow! You've got to help me!'

'Josh?'

CHAPTER THIRTY-TWO
PATSY

Patsy left her breakfast dishes in the sink. She had lost all motivation to tackle them, and besides, she wasn't here to clean. She was here to find Josh. It was already baking as she headed outside, and she wished she had packed a hat.

Kelly's kiosk was open. Patsy recognised Kelly instantly, hard at work scrubbing everything down. Her face looked more lined than it had online. Her eyes were more crinkly, and her nose more hooked. She must have been using a beauty filter.

She marched towards her, determined to have it out with her. Why hadn't Kelly called her when things started to go wrong? Why hadn't she mentioned Hugo's accident?

Without looking up, or acknowledging her, Kelly started talking.

'Someone broke into my house last night.'

She struggled to make sense of what Kelly was saying. She felt derailed somehow.

'How awful. Did they take much?'

'They didn't take anything, but they were in my home, touching my things. I have never felt so violated.'

'I'm sorry about that. That must have been horrible. Listen, it's so nice to finally meet you in person. I really need your help. You've been watching the kids, observing. Where did Josh go every day? Did he have any particular habits? Anything that might have been missed?'

Kelly thought for a minute. 'Well, he always ordered a bacon roll and coffee from me in the mornings.'

'Did he do that on the day he went missing?'

'I can't say. I had to go to the market, so I left my assistant in charge. He can't remember if he saw Josh or not. To be honest, he's not the sharpest tool in the box.'

She nodded, trying to keep her frustration under control.

'Did you see him talking to anyone while he was here? Did he make any friends?'

'He talked to anyone and everyone. Ask the ladies from the aqua aerobics class! But he was with his sister and his friends, mostly. Whenever I saw one of them, the others weren't far behind. Except for the day the girls went off to Sozopol. I didn't see much of any of them that day.'

Patsy nodded. It felt so weird to be finally talking to Kelly in person. She wasn't at all how she had found her online. There was a skittishness to her that hadn't come across on Facebook. She was both friendly but guarded, kindly but neurotic. What was it with the constant scrubbing and cleaning? And why wouldn't she look at her properly? It was as if she was afraid to look her in the eyes.

Kelly reached out and grabbed her hand in what might be construed as a comforting gesture, except her grip was a little too tight. Patsy fought the urge to shake her off. She didn't want to offend this woman. She had been here. She might know something.

'I really do understand how you're feeling,' Kelly said. 'At least, I have some idea.'

'Oh?'

The Beach

'I never told you my truth, did I? About what happened to my son, Pierce?'

Patsy shook her head. Although she had picked up enough from the old newspaper reports, she couldn't tell Kelly that. Besides, she wanted to hear it in Kelly's own words.

'He came here on holiday with his friends. He had never been abroad before. Neither of us had. I had a terrible feeling as I waved him off. I felt so sad, like I was never going to see him again. I told myself I was being silly. You have to let them go some time, don't you? But I was right. He never came home.'

'What happened?'

'He was with his friends in the villa. The same one your kids are staying in, in fact. I'd spoken to him just the day before. He had been having so much fun, drinking, partying, doing all the things young people do. No one was watching when he fell from the balcony. Pierce was a strong swimmer, but the fall must have disorientated him. They found him lying at the bottom of the pool.'

Patsy swallowed hard. 'How awful!'

All at once, Kelly was looking at her, her eyes wild and unblinking.

'I cannot tell you, Patsy, how angry I feel about that, that no one was looking out for him. That's why I wanted to be the guardian Pierce never had. And I can't tell you how sorry I am that I have failed you. I am wracked with guilt and grief. But I promise you that I will continue to keep an eye out for Josh. If I hear one word of a whisper, any rumours, I will pass them on to you. I promise you, Patsy. We will find him.'

Patsy nodded. Her wrist was starting to ache.

'Do you know a local girl called Elizaveta? Josh was supposed to be with her when he went missing.'

'Oh yes, the family does lots of odd jobs around the resort. Elizaveta included, but she and her friends like to hang out with the tourists. Sometimes they take them on tours, especially the handsome boys, like your son.'

'Do you think that's what happened? She took Josh on a tour?'

She thought of Spence's fall from the cliffs and shuddered.

'I never actually saw them together, and she likes to show off, Elizaveta. But she never came by with Josh. I didn't even know they knew each other until Tiana mentioned it. Tiana didn't look very happy about it. I think she was jealous.'

'Yes, well, Tiana's had a crush on Josh for as long as I can remember.'

Patsy glanced at her watch. The police divers would be getting ready at the harbour. They had already done a preliminary search of the water, but today it would be getting more serious. They weren't expecting to find him alive. She understood that much. They were looking for his body.

Kelly finally let go of her wrist so that she could fill a bag with food and drinks for her, and she pointed out which path to take. Patsy thanked her and hurried away. Sad as her story was, there was something unsettling about that woman.

As she walked, she tried not to think about the purpose of this morning's expedition. They would not find Josh. She was certain of it. It made more sense to her that he had been abducted. Especially since Willow had received that odd text claiming to be him. She had forgotten to ask Grigoriev about whether there was going to be a press conference. As far as she knew, there hadn't been one so far and it would definitely help put Josh's disappearance in the spotlight. She wasn't exactly enthusiastic about speaking in front of a load of cameras, but she would have the chance to speak to him directly, to let him know that she was here, and that she would never give up. Not to mention the chance to plead with his captor to let him go.

The path Kelly had shown her was longer than it had looked on the map. Patsy was a good walker, but she began to wish she had taken a bus. She was going to be knackered by the time she got down there.

As she passed one of the houses, she saw a young woman out the front, practicing her tennis serve up against the wall. She had long dark hair all the way down to her waist. Her spine tingled. Could it be…

The woman caught her looking. She walked over to her, almost as if she had been expecting her.

'You are Josh's mother?'

'Yes.'

'Are you Elizaveta?'

Elizaveta nodded and cast a quick glance behind her, as if she was afraid of being overheard. She leaned over the fence.

'I must speak with you.'

She dropped her racquet and began to jog down the path, so that she was a little way in front of Patsy. In her white tennis clothes and baseball cap, she looked like she was out for a jog.

Patsy followed. Elizaveta was heading in the direction she had been going, towards the harbour.

'What is it you want to tell me?' she asked, struggling to keep up.

'Not here. Follow me. Don't let anybody see.'

A COUPLE of people appeared on the footpath ahead, and Elizaveta's jog became a sprint. Patsy puffed and panted, trying to keep up. Elizaveta waited until they had passed, then slowed her pace. Patsy caught up to her and fought the urge to grab her arm. If she knew something, there was no way she was letting her out of her sight.

They walked through a field and down towards the sea. It must be a shortcut. She could see boats bobbing about in the water, yachts and fishing vessels moored side by side.

He can't be in the water. He just can't.

There were food shacks and vans down there. The sun blared brightly and people were buying seafood and ice-cream, some posing for pictures in front of the boats.

Further, they went, passed all the hubbub, until they reached a quiet area where there were office buildings and car parks. And then she saw the shipping containers, and it struck her that this was the perfect place to hide a captive.

She watched as Elizaveta walked up to one of the containers and tapped twice. When there was no response, she turned the door handle. It opened and she peered inside. Then she came out again. She nodded her head.

Patsy's heart beat fast as she followed her lead. She was terrified and excited at the same time. She opened the door and looked inside. It was dark in there, but she could make out someone lying on a mattress. She felt for a light, but there wasn't one. She stepped inside and listened. She could hear shallow breathing.

'Hello?' she whispered. 'Josh?'

She reached out and touched flesh. There was a small noise. She recognised the moan.

She pulled back the cover, but it wasn't Josh. It was Willow. There was a gag over her mouth, her arms tied behind her. Her eyes were wide and frightened. She gesticulated to the door behind her. Patsy swung round, but she was too late. The door slammed shut and clicked into place. They were trapped.

CHAPTER THIRTY-THREE
PATSY

Patsy threw herself against the door, but when it refused to open, she pounded on it hard and shouted for help. She yelled and banged for several minutes, but no one came. She turned back to her daughter and freed her of the gag, then set to work on the ropes that secured her arms.

'Willow, what happened?'

Willow drew a breath of air. 'Josh is alive. He phoned me.'

Patsy's heart stopped in her chest. She felt a surge of adrenaline rush through her veins, igniting sparks in her brain like a wildfire.

'Are you certain it was Josh? What did he say?'

'He said… "You've got to help me! Someone locked me in a shipping container. It's the one with the green door. Let me out."

'I was practically standing in front of it, Mum. I didn't think about that at the time, how he could have possibly known I was there? I just opened the door and the next thing I knew, I was being shoved inside. I think I lost consciousness for a bit, and when I woke up, I was tied up.'

'But it was Josh on the phone? You're sure of it?'

Willow sighed. 'It sounded really echoey, but it was him, Mum. He's alive.'

Patsy took a moment to take this in. In spite of their current predicament, she felt an overwhelming sense of peace. Her boy was alive. Josh was not dead. He was not in the water.

'So where is he?' she asked, looking around the empty container.

'I don't know. I've felt like someone was watching me all week. I thought I was being paranoid. And that wasn't his phone he rang from. It was someone else's.'

'They used him to get us,' Patsy said grimly. She shone her phone around, scanning the space. But there was nothing to see except the mattress Willow was sitting on. No sign Josh had ever been there.

'How did you find me?'

'It was Elizaveta. She led me down here. She seemed scared. I don't think she's behind all this. I think she's just a puppet.'

Willow nodded. 'Spence wrote a poem about a friend who wasn't a friend,' she said, pulling out the book.

Patsy read the words grimly.

'I think I know who it is.' She sat down next to Willow on the mattress. 'Last night, I saw Hugo in the kitchen and he wasn't using his crutches. He was walking around perfectly fine. His leg was never broken, Willow. He's been faking it. Which means he could have been up to anything, couldn't he?'

'You're kidding!'

'I wish. He's been playing us this whole time.'

'But why?'

'I have no idea. I think he's jealous of Josh, because he's so popular with the girls.'

'What about Spence? Do you…you think he pushed him?'

'That would explain why he's pretending to have a broken

leg. No one would suspect poor old Hugo. He could easily have slipped out and followed you up that cliff.'

Willow frowned. 'But it wasn't Hugo who lured you down here. It was Elizaveta. She doesn't even know Hugo.'

'Maybe he paid her.'

'You said she looked scared?'

'He could have threatened her in some way? I don't know. It's so strange. I think someone must have told Josh to call you. They wanted us here. Both of us. But why? Do you think they are going to take us to Josh?'

She felt hopeful, even if she was about to die. Seeing Josh one more time would be worth it. Right now, she wanted to see him more than anything in the entire world.

She looked down at her phone again. It was out of range. She stood and walked all around the shipping container until finally...

'Yes! I've got a signal! Who do I call?'

'999!'

Patsy nodded. It made sense, since she didn't know the Bulgarian emergency number. The phone call connected.

'Emergency. Which service do you require? Fire, police or ambulance?'

'Help...I need the police. We've been kidnapped. We're in...Hello? Damit, I've lost the signal!'

Willow stared at her. 'Did you feel that?'

'What?'

'We're moving.'

PATSY WOBBLED. The ground she was standing on was shaking and sliding about.

'Help!' Willow yelled, banging on the wall of the container. 'Help! We're in here! We're locked in!'

They waited, but nobody responded.

'How much air is in here?'

'It's fine', Patsy said, with more certainty than she felt. 'Just keep breathing. Try not to panic.'

'I can't help it!'

They both pounded on the walls, over and over, but to no avail. No one was coming.

They tried their phones again, but the signal was gone.

'Maybe that call was enough.' Patsy said. 'Maybe they'll be able to trace us.'

But as they continued to move, she felt less certain. It felt like they were being transported somewhere, on a lorry, perhaps. Or worse still, out to sea.

CHAPTER THIRTY-FOUR
PATSY

Patsy squirmed on the lumpy mattress, trying to find a comfortable spot among the springs poking through the thin fabric. Her stomach churned and twisted as she lay in the dim container. With zero bathroom facilities, they'd had to use the carrier bag Kelly had given them as a toilet. Thankfully, there had been a few napkins at the bottom of the bag, so they could clean up.

She looked over at her daughter, her heart breaking at the sight of her exhausted form. After being sick multiple times, Willow had finally drifted off to sleep.

Thank god for Kelly. Without her thoughtfulness, they would have no supplies at all.

The packets of biscuits and crisps rolled around as the ship tilted. She had tried lining them up in one corner, but the movement of the waves kept shifting things. It was the water she was most concerned with. They only had two bottles. Plus one can of Coke and another of lemonade.

Whoever had locked them in clearly didn't care about the consequences.

'Can I have a bit more water?' Willow asked, opening one eye.

Patsy handed her the bottle they'd started on.

'Don't drink it all at once. We don't know how long we might be stuck in here.'

'Do you think they'll be waiting for us, whoever did this? When we get to wherever we're going?'

'No,' Patsy said grimly.

They would assume they were dead.

THEY PLAYED word association games to pass the time and shared stories about the good times with Josh. The time he won the talent contest at primary school with his rubbish magic trick.

'I think the teachers just felt sorry for him,' Patsy said with a smile.

'He had them all wrapped around his little finger,' Willow remembered. She hadn't been too happy about it at the time. She and Tiana had put a lot of effort into their song and dance routine, but everyone said Josh was adorable, so Josh had won.

Patsy's phone died, then Willow's.

With nothing much to do, they both laid down to conserve energy. It was a terrible time, and yet it was the most time Patsy had spent with Willow since she was tiny. Willow talked about her feelings for Spence.

'I was so frustrated with him,' she admitted. 'He kept pressuring me to move in with him. He was always so bloody intense, Mum. I don't know for sure, but I think it's possible he might have jumped.'

Patsy stared at her. 'Surely not? He had everything to live for.'

'I'm not sure he saw it that way. I think he thought if we weren't going to be together, then he just couldn't cope.'

Patsy reached for her daughter and held her while she cried. 'Even if he did jump, and I'm not saying that's true, that would have been his decision, Willow. Nothing to do with you. You can't live other people's lives for them. You can't force them to make rational decisions. You can only do the best you can at the time.'

THEY TALKED about everything during those long, drawn out days. Willow told her about what had happened at Kelly's, how disturbing it had been to find that body.

'The worst part is that it took me right back to what happened to Dad.'

Patsy felt herself stiffen. Even after all these years, she found it very hard to think about that day, let alone talk about it.

'I've always felt such guilt,' Willow admitted. 'That we didn't do enough to save him.'

Patsy shook her head. 'You were just little children. You weren't to know. And besides, he had suffered a massive heart attack. There was nothing you could have done.'

But even she wondered why neither of them had thought to call an ambulance. She thought she had taught them that much. How to dial 999 and ask for help.

'It must have been the shock,' Willow said. 'I think we both knew he was gone, and we couldn't bear for them to come and take him away. We were just waiting, really. Waiting for you to come back home.'

Patsy swallowed hard. She would never admit it in a thousand years, but she had been angry that Willow hadn't made that call. She had been the older one, the more responsible of the two.

They all had to live with the consequences of that weekend, her children growing up without their dad, her without her husband. She remembered the restless nights when Willow would wake up crying, and when Josh would wet the bed.

'Do you think we'll all be together again when we die?' Willow asked.

Patsy pulled her closer. 'I really hope so. I would like that so, so much.'

For hours on end, they lay in the cramped space, their muscles aching from lack of movement. Patsy stared up at the ceiling as her eyes grew bleary with exhaustion. She desperately tried to find something to distract her from the suffocating walls that seemed to close in tighter and tighter by the minute. Her mind yearned for a glimpse of blue sky or even a whiff of fresh air, but all she could sense was the stale, musty scent of the enclosed space.

She couldn't help but wonder if this was what it felt like to lose your grip on reality. Despite their best efforts to ration their dwindling supplies of food and water, they were soon left with nothing. They lay side by side on the thin mattress. For much of the time, they were hot and sweaty, with no way of getting fresh air into the stifling container. All Patsy could think about was Josh. She longed for the impossible - to have both her children with her, safe and sound.

Then a voice cut through the stillness of the container.

'Mum!' Patsy opened one eye. Willow was shaking her. Her face was lit up with excitement.

'What is it?'

'Mum, I heard something. It sounded like a horn. And there were voices. I think we're coming into land.'

CHAPTER THIRTY-FIVE
PATSY

They were so weak, but they crawled to the sides of the container and pounded their fists against the hot metal walls. Their voices echoed back at them in loud, mocking taunts.

'Help! Help, let us out!'

Then the container door creaked opened to reveal a group of men, their expressions a mix of confusion and alarm.

Willow's legs gave way beneath her as she collapsed into sobs of relief. One of the men stepped forward to help her out.

'Thank you! Thank you!' Patsy cried.

They lay on the dock like exhausted seals, taking in deep gulps of the fresh briny air. The tangy scent filled their lungs and washed away the suffocating stench of sweaty air and desperation. Patsy didn't care where they were, only that they were finally safe from the confines of their dark, metal prison.

'The ambulance is on its way,' someone told her in perfect English. But the others were speaking excitedly in a different language. Patsy took a moment to tune in. It sounded like German.

The police met them at the hospital where they were both

treated for dehydration, their skin clinging to their bones after so many days at sea. Her heart raced as she recounted their harrowing journey and asked for news of Josh.

'Please check the other shipping containers. He might be inside one.'

Willow looked at her. 'Do you think he could have made it?'

'That's all I can hope,' Patsy said.

She could still feel the motion of the sea rocking her to and fro, and when she closed her eyes, she was still trapped inside that shipping container. She couldn't bear to think of her son, starved and alone, tossing around like cargo in his own metal box.

She waited anxiously for news. After all this, what if they told her Josh had died? She didn't think she could bear it.

The police left and her phone beeped. She had got one of the nurses to plug in a charger in case Josh tried to contact them. She peered at her messages. There were dozens of them, mainly from Misha, one from her optician, and one from her boss, but that was it.

She exhaled. Where was he?

Willow's phone also sprang to life, but she didn't have any messages from Josh either.

'He did call me,' she insisted. 'I know it was him.'

'I believe you,' Patsy said.

The police returned that afternoon. A short, stout woman with a tightly pursed mouth and a taller, more jovial one who handed her a box of Yorkshire Tea.

'I'm sure you must be in need of a good cuppa.'

'Thank you,' Patsy said with a smile.

'How are you feeling?'

'Much better, thank you.'

'The doctors say you were both seriously dehydrated. They think you'll make a full recovery, but another twenty-four hours and it might have been a very different story.'

'Yes, I know.'

She had been told they would need to remain in hospital for a few more days, but they wouldn't be able to leave Germany just yet, anyway. She had been on the phone to the British consulate, who were helping to get them papers so they could travel back to England, since their passports and other belongings were still in Paradise Palms.

'I'm afraid we did not find your son in any of the containers on the ship you were on,' the tall policewoman told her. 'The Bulgarian police are continuing to locate and search other ships that left the port around the same time, but so far, no luck.'

'What about CCTV?'

'They are still gathering what they can, but the coverage around the harbour is patchy.'

'And there have been no sightings of Josh?'

'Not as yet.'

'What about Elizaveta? Have the police spoken to her?'

'I will have to pass that question over to the police in Bulgaria. I'll get them to update you on that.'

Patsy nodded. 'She seemed frightened, I thought. I distinctly remember how she kept looking behind her. Someone was watching her, I'm sure of it. They were also watching Willow when she got the phone call from Josh.'

Both policewomen nodded gravely.

'But if Josh is not in another container, then where is he? Could he still be in Bulgaria?'

The stout policewoman shook her head. 'It's hard to say. This is an unusual case. Highly unusual. I can't think of another one quite like it. All of you abducted. And for what end? It makes no sense. No ransom has been demanded, has it?'

'I certainly didn't receive one.'

She wished she had.

'Right. Well, we are now waiting on the arrival of Detective Grigoryev from Bulgaria. He will update us on how things are going there. They are checking more shipping containers, in and out of the port. I must say, they are being very thorough.'

She sounded surprised by this, as if she expected sloppy police work.

'And the divers found nothing?' Patsy asked.

'That is a question for him.'

After they left, Willow received a text from Radoslav, updating her on Kelly's case. Apparently, Kelly had been dealt with quietly, with compassion. He confirmed there was no link to be found with Josh's disappearance.

Detective Grigoryev arrived the following day. He had dark circles under his eyes, and his suit was even more creased than it had been the last time she had seen him.

'We found your son's phone in the water. It's ruined, of course. There are no prints or other useful data, but it's definitely his phone.'

Patsy tried to remain composed, but her hands trembled. This was not the news she wanted to hear. But it was a phone, not a body. She tried to stay calm.

'Is there anyone else you think might be involved?' he asked.

'Hugo Pickering-Jones,' Willow said. 'He's my friend, but Spence was suspicious of him, and my mum saw him walk without crutches when he was supposed to be injured. Can you at least question him?'

'Where is he?'

'He went home.'

'To England?'

'Yes.'

'In that case, we will have to go through the British police. Hopefully that won't be a problem.'

The Beach

PATSY'S PHONE rang off the hook. The journalists she'd spoken to about Josh were keen to remind her of their connection. She agreed to speak to them both over the phone about the ordeal she and Willow had been through, and she agreed to send them photos. Any publicity was good publicity, she reasoned, since she needed to keep Josh's name in the papers.

Social media blew up with the story, largely thanks to Tiana, who seemed to have nothing better to do than spam Instagram. Willow showed her how much she had been posting since they went missing. It seemed incredible that so many people had liked or commented on Tiana's posts, and they still weren't any closer to finding Josh.

Detective Grigoryev came back to see them the following day, just as Patsy had awoken from her nap. No matter how much she slept, she still felt bone tired.

'There's no evidence Hugo's involved, I'm afraid. The MET police in London brought him in for questioning, but didn't manage to get anything out of him. Either he's a very convincing liar or he's innocent.'

'Right, thank you,' Patsy said. She wasn't sure whether to be pleased or relieved. It had been unpleasant to imagine Josh being tricked by one of his best friends, but somebody had to be responsible.

'What about him faking his injury?'

Grigoriev shrugged. 'That's hardly a criminal matter. I suggest you talk to him about that yourself once you get back to England.'

'And what about Elizaveta?'

'We would like to question her in light of the part she played in your abduction, but at present that is not possible.'

'Why not?'

'It appears she has absconded.'

'What do you mean?'

'Her parents say she left a note and ran off.'

Patsy sat up straight. 'No, I'm telling you, that girl was scared. Whoever took Josh, I think they were using her, making her do things she didn't want to. That's why she lured me down to the shipping container.'

Grigoriev tapped his pen against the table. 'Her parents say she is high spirited and popular. She doesn't sound like the kind of person who would be easily manipulated.'

'I was there. I saw the fear in her eyes. Please, look into it. If Elizaveta is missing, she may be a victim too.'

CHAPTER THIRTY-SIX
PATSY

It was raining the day after Patsy and Willow arrived back in England. Patsy stood by the patio doors, enjoying the relief of the cool rain falling on the garden. The droplets danced on the leaves and petals, nourishing plants that had struggled during her unexpected absence. She'd come back to find them all wilted and shrivelled, all except the roses Josh had given her for her last birthday. Against all the odds, they had prospered, their velvety petals reaching out for the sky. She hoped to show them to him when he finally came home.

Her thoughts were interrupted by the chime of the doorbell. She shot Willow a questioning glance and went to peer through the spyhole. It was Hugo. He had Tiana with him. She suspected that was simply to put them at their ease. Her gut twisted as she remembered that last night in Paradise Palms. The way Hugo had walked around the kitchen without his crutches. The way he had looked at her. Could they have missed something?

He pressed the bell a second time. Perhaps she should speak to him, see if she could get information out of him.

'I just want to see Willow,' he said. 'I was so worried.'

'We both were,' Tiana said.

Patsy looked at both of them carefully. 'Alright then, come on through. She's in the living room. But just for a bit, okay? She needs her rest. We both do.'

Hugo's leg was evidently all better now. He made no reference to it and walked over to the sofa with perfect ease. He kept looking at Willow with puppy dog eyes and she realised with a thud that he was interested in her. She wasn't sure if Willow had noticed. She was still cut up about Spence.

'What I don't understand is how the police still haven't found Josh,' Tiana said. 'Or Elizaveta, for that matter. I knew she was no good. You should have let me pummel her while I had the chance.'

Willow shook her head and told them what they knew about the police investigation. Tiana asked lots of questions, but Hugo said very little. He didn't mention the fact that he had been questioned. Was that because he was hiding something, or was he just embarrassed?

Patsy rose to her feet.

'Hugo, would you mind helping me in the kitchen for a minute?' she asked.

He looked a bit startled, then stood and followed her out of the room.

'How's your leg?'

'Much better, thanks.'

'Hmm. Well, you know, back at the villa, I saw you walking around without your crutches.'

A sly look slid across his face. 'Turns out my leg wasn't actually broken.'

She tilted her head. 'Didn't you have an X-ray?'

He glanced out at the living room. 'It's just that, after the accident, Willow was so sweet to me. She stopped looking at me like something she had stepped in and seemed to actually care. It felt good. I genuinely was in a lot of pain. It was a really nasty accident. I don't know if you heard what happened, but something snapped on my kiteboard and I just spun out of control. I've never been so scared in my life. Seriously, I thought I was going to die. I was in total agony. I couldn't believe it when I went for the x-ray and they couldn't see a fracture. I know this is going to sound ridiculous, but if my leg had been broken, I would have felt vindicated. Like, yes, I had the right to act like a baby because I was in so much pain.

I think the hospital staff understood how I was feeling because the nurse said I could have it put in plaster if I wanted, just to be on the safe side. So I agreed. I didn't lie. I never said my leg was broken, everyone just assumed. After a couple of days, it felt a lot better. All the swelling went down and it felt more normal again. I just didn't know how to tell the others, especially Willow. She had been so nice to me, and what with Josh going missing, she had more important things to worry about. And yes, I did feel like a total fraud.'

He looked up at her through his lashes. 'You won't say anything, will you? I'd be mortified.'

Despite his supposed mortification, there was a slight glint in his eye that made Patsy's skin crawl. He looked pleased with himself, she thought. As if he thought he was pulling the wool over her eyes.

She shifted her weight from one foot to the other, a nervous energy pulsing through her.

'Right, well, I suppose I should check on the biscuits. Would you mind passing me those oven gloves?'

He did as she asked, standing a little too close as she opened the oven. Heat radiated onto her skin, adding to the beads of sweat forming on her forehead. She took a deep breath, trying to calm her nerves as she pulled the sheet of biscuits out and placed it on top of the cooker to cool.

'I'm surprised you're up to baking already,' he said.

'Oh no, my friend Misha left them for me.'

Misha seemed to think biscuits were vital to their recovery.

That and a huge care package of VivaLux bath products. Patsy would have preferred a casserole. Still her heart was in the right place.

She took the oven gloves and pulled the biscuits out. They smelled delicious, like spicy ginger.

'Josh used to love these,' Hugo said.

Patsy gripped the end of the table. 'He still does.'

'Yes. Yes, of course.'

She slid the hot biscuits onto a plate.

'Can you bring out the lemonade?'

They walked back to the living room, where Willow and Tiana sat huddled together on the sofa. Patsy suspected they'd been talking about Hugo.

She poured the drinks and they ate the biscuits. Then everyone went quiet, presumably thinking about Josh. And possibly Spence. It seemed incredible. That six of them had gone on holiday and only four came back.

Hugo broke the silence by talking about some trick Josh had learnt, somersaulting backwards into the pool and splashing everyone in the process.

'Yeah, that was peak Josh,' Tiana said, wiping tears from her eyes.

Hugo drifted over to the fireplace, where all the family pictures hung: Willow and Josh at their first cricket match. Willow and Josh joining the scouts. Even their school pictures showed them together. It was a small school, and they'd been in the same classes all the way through. She bristled as he ran his fingers over the glass frame of a picture of Josh and Willow on a sail boat.

'I'd rather you didn't touch that,' she said, a little more sharply than she had meant to.

He inched away. 'Oh, sorry. I was just looking.'

'That lemonade has gone right through me. I'm just going to the loo,' Tiana said, getting to her feet.

She clomped up the stairs.

The Beach

Hugo took the chance to sit down next to Willow. 'What are you going to do now, then?' he asked. 'Tiana said you'd jacked in your job?'

'Yeah, well, I realised it wasn't for me,' she said with a shrug.

She would have to find another job, eventually. Patsy couldn't afford to support her indefinitely, but now was not the time to talk about that.

'What are you going to do?' Willow asked him.

'I don't know. I was planning to go travelling but my parents aren't keen after what happened to Josh. They want me to stay close to home until it's time to leave for uni.'

'Have you seen Lia at all?'

'No, but my mum figured out why she wanted to go to Sunderland instead of Reading.'

'Why?'

'Apparently, she failed her exams and she was too embarrassed to tell anyone.'

'Damn!'

'She got the place at Sunderland through the clearing process. It's a good course, but obviously miles from home. I think she's been trying to justify it to herself these last few weeks. This idea that she needs to move away from us all, to reinvent herself.'

Patsy raised an eyebrow. Lia and Willow had always been so close. It felt strange to be hearing all this from Hugo, rather than Lia herself.

'Do you think that's why she went so weird?'

He looked down at his hands. 'I think she's been having a bit of an identity crisis lately. I wouldn't take it personally. Let her go off and see who she wants to be. She might come back to us, after she's figured herself out a bit.'

Willow leaned her head on his shoulder. 'How did you get so wise?'

Patsy couldn't bear to watch any longer. It occurred to her

that Tiana had been in the bathroom a long time. Perhaps she should go and check on her? She headed up the stairs. The bathroom door was wide open. Tiana wasn't in there. She crossed the hall, and there she was, sitting on Josh's bed. She was clutching something in her hand. A small, handwoven bracelet. He had made it the summer he was thirteen. They'd been all the rage back then. He and Willow had made tons of those bracelets. They'd had a little business going, selling them on the playground at school until the teachers put a stop to it. He must have kept this one. She watched as Tiana slipped it into her pocket.

She let her have it. After all, it was just a bracelet.

She slipped back downstairs. Hugo's arm was resting casually on the arm of Willow's armchair. It made her uncomfortable. Spence hadn't even been buried yet.

She cleared her throat, but still Hugo did not withdraw his hand. It irked her, the way he was moving in on Willow. She was vulnerable right now. She didn't need him complicating things.

Her phone chirped and she leapt on it, as she always did these days. There was a new message from Kelly:

Word is, Elizaveta's been in contact with her mother. She says she's coming home.

CHAPTER THIRTY-SEVEN
WILLOW

The rain poured down in a relentless curtain as they gathered at the summit of Salisbury Hill. Spence's closest friends and family formed a tight circle, huddled together against the chill.

Everyone was holding a candle and Tom went around, lighting them all with some difficulty because of the wind and the rain.

His voice trembled with emotion as he spoke:

'Spence, we will never forget you. We live our lives to honour your memory. We won't waste a day.'

His words hung heavy in the misty air, carried by the howling wind. Together, they walked round in a solemn circle. The candles danced wildly, but none went out. They brought their candles together so that they were one bright flame that lit up the dark sky. They held it there while the wind and rain attacked from above. Their English teacher read one of Spence's best poems. There was power in those words. The rain seemed to intensify, almost as if it too mourned the loss of a friend.

There would be no gravestone, no wreath. Spence would hate all of that. He wouldn't even like the phrase "Rest in peace." He was a tortured soul, a poet, consumed by darkness. Pain was his fuel, his muse. He had welcomed it.

'He's going to haunt us, isn't he?' Hugo murmured in Willow's ear.

Willow tilted her head slightly and met his gaze. 'I hope so.'

Her mum shot her a look. She didn't think she should get so cosy with Hugo. She thought it was insensitive to Spence's family. But Willow needed her friends right now. She was so hurt and confused. There was still no news of Josh. The world had forgotten him. Everyone was starting new jobs or going off to uni, and she was left behind, waiting for her brother.

People asked her about Josh and she wished she had something to tell them. She supposed no news was good news. There had been some excitement when Elizaveta's family claimed to have heard from her, but days passed and still their daughter was not home. Willow wondered if someone had scared her off.

She and Tiana had been busy making a book out of Spence's poetry. They were selling it to raise money for teens who got into trouble abroad. Spence hadn't believed in getting commercial gain for his words, but he would have liked to help people, she was sure of that.

She didn't need to look at the book to remember the poem she wanted to recite. She knew it by heart:

> You will not see me in the morning.
> As the dawn breaks, I'll be gone.
> You may wonder why I left you.
> You may wonder where I've gone.
> You will not see me in the morning
> Though I wish I could be there.
> You may hear me whisper,
> In your heart, where I belong
> I will be there deep inside you,

The Beach

> Forever anchored, forever yours,
> As the sun breaks through with gentle grace,
> Let my light shine on,
> You will not see me in the morning.
> In the morning, I'll be gone.

WHEN THE CEREMONY WAS OVER, she helped Tom gather up the flowers and tributes people had left. He was much thinner than the last time she had seen him, and he looked as though his chin would collapse beneath the weight of his smile.

'We'll press the flowers,' she suggested. 'I can put them all in a book, along with the notes and cards.'

'Thank you, that sounds nice.'

When she got home, Willow sat in her room, sifting through it all; cards from teachers and friends. Spence had never been popular. His personality was too spikey, too adversarial. He was often misunderstood. But all the notes were kind and positive, full of regret that he was gone, and they contained an eclectic sprinkling of memories. One in particular caught her eye. A postcard postmarked 'Paradise Palms'.

She peered at the writing. There was something familiar about that square, boxy scrawl:

The front showed a picture of a couple relaxing on a sun lounger at the beach. The picture of perfect contentment. The perfect holiday. She stared at it for a moment, taking in the vivid blue waters of the sea, the pale yellow sand. Her eyes traced over the delicate loops and curves of the flowing red ink, the i's dotted with hearts:

You're in a better place, mate.
A place where you don't have to set an alarm.
You get to sleep as long as you want!
No one can tell you what to do.

You're living the dream, mate.
Wish I was living it with you.

She got up from her chair and went downstairs to the living room. There on the mantlepiece sat the postcard she had scribbled to her mum:

She turned it over. Her own writing was in blue biro. She too had dotted the I's with hearts:

This is such an amazing place, Mum!
So great, not having to set an alarm!
We get to sleep as long as we want!
Thinking of you spending all day at work,
We're totally living the dream, Mum!
Wish you were here!
Willow and Josh xxx

CHAPTER THIRTY-EIGHT
JOSH

The boat rose and fell with the relentless rhythm of the ocean, twisting and turning in the waves. Josh clutched his stomach, feeling queasy and light-headed. He knew it wouldn't be long before he succumbed to seasickness again. It seemed like a cruel irony - there had been a time when he had longed to live on a boat, thinking it would be the ultimate luxury and adventure. He had always been drawn to the water, mesmerised by the constant movement of the waves. But now, after so many days at sea, he was desperate to see solid ground again. He leaned over the side, wishing there was a way to make it stop spinning and rocking so violently. The salty spray stung his face as he closed his eyes and prayed for land to appear on the horizon.

The storm raged on, tossing him back and forth. He grasped at the side as a particularly powerful wave threw him back and his head cracked painfully against the rough surface.

Moaning and cursing, he massaged the throbbing spot on his temple. Thunder boomed overhead like a war drum, and rain pounded down like a barrage of bullets. He knew he should go back into the cabin, but the enclosed space made his sickness worse. At least here he could feel the fresh air on his face.

He squinted through the blur towards the open sea. This life was nothing like he had imagined. There was nothing romantic about this.

He thought about his old life back in England. His friends, his mother, and even Willow flooded his mind. He couldn't help but smile as he remembered how she used to boss him around, thinking she was in charge just because she was eleven months older. It felt strange knowing he would never see her again.

His gaze drifted over to the old-fashioned radio perched on the bench next to him. It was a relic from a bygone era, but somehow, it felt comforting in its simplicity. He had never been one for listening to the radio, always preferring to curate his own playlist. With a flick of his finger, he switched it on. The soft crackle of static gave way to a clear voice delivering the latest news. And as he listened, he felt a sense of connection to the outside world, even if it was just through this small device.

It took a few minutes to find an English language station. It was soothing, listening to this voice, talking to him through the airwaves. He had never really taken much interest in events outside his own country's borders, but now he found himself drawn in as the voice updated him on the latest events all around the globe. He couldn't help but wonder why the world seemed to be in a constant state of chaos. So much fighting, so much war.

Right at the end of the segment, the newsreaders' voice lifted a little, as if to give the listeners hope.

'And this just in. Two British women were found alive in a shipping container in Germany. It appears the women were forced into the container near Burgas, Bulgaria. Against all odds, the women have survived, despite having spent over a week at sea with limited food and water. They are now being treated in a local hospital for severe dehydration. Another member of their family, an eighteen-year-old male, is still missing.'

His heart beat a little faster. Him! They were talking about him!

'Joshua Spicer has been missing since the 22nd of August. He is described a slim, 5ft 11 with blond hair.'

He leaned back in his seat, not caring as a wave soaked him.

Mum and Willow were alive. They had made it.

Another wave lashed over the side of the boat, splashing him from head to toe. He looked down at his soaked T-shirt. He was still in shock, he realised, taking in the news.

They were alive. Tears rolled down his face as he processed this information. His heart throbbed with confusion. He threw his head back, the sound of his laughter echoing around the deck, wild and unconstrained. He felt it deep in his chest. They were alive! Against all odds. The rush of adrenaline and disbelief overwhelmed him. He stared out at the treacherous sea and laughed again, manically and uncontrollably.

He didn't even notice when Elizaveta emerged from the cabin.

'You should come inside. You're getting soaked.'

He clenched his jaw. 'Have you heard? About my mum and Willow? They've been found alive.'

She stared at him. 'How is this possible?'

'I don't know.'

He rose from his seat and made his way towards her, not caring about the waves tossing him about.

'It's all your fault,' he snarled, grabbing her by the shoulders and shaking her violently. 'You didn't do your job properly.'

'I did! I did exactly as you said.'

He raised his hand and struck her across the cheek. The sound echoed through the air like a gunshot.

'It's all your fault.'

CHAPTER THIRTY-NINE
JOSH

Four months earlier

Josh placed the brochure on the doormat with the rest of the post. He smiled to himself as he walked back through the house and settled in the kitchen with a cup of coffee. His mother was sitting in the living room, looking at her laptop. Supposedly she was checking her work emails but really, she was browsing her newsfeed.

Ever so casually, he got up and stood behind her chair. Sure enough, she was looking at Facebook. She scrolled right past the first ad and spent a few minutes browsing, replying to her friends' status updates and liking all their cat memes. Misha was spamming everyone with her posts about VivaLux, getting her friends to sign up to be consultants, or else purchase cosmetics from her. It was ironic, really. She was making him a tidy profit, and she had no idea she even worked for him.

Patsy had warned Misha against the company in a private message. She was a bit more savvy, his mum. She understood that VivaLux was basically a pyramid scheme, but fortunately Misha wouldn't listen. She had worked her way up to

Diamond consultant status and there was no way she was giving that up.

Patsy was scrolling again. Ah, there it was, his other advert. He had used a different image for this one. It did the trick. She gazed at it, taking in the details. Paradise Palms resort. With its brilliant blue water and white sands. A close up of the swimming pool. Quiet. Affordable. Safe.

Perfect. She was nicely primed.

Any minute, Willow would be seeing the ads he had run to her Instagram feed. He had emphasised cheap cocktails. Willow liked a bargain. Dance parties. Culture. After seeing the ads repeatedly, the idea would take hold in her head.

They were going to Bulgaria. It was a done deal.

'Hey Josh? Do you have a minute?'

Willow's voice was eager as she approached him, her eyes sparkling with excitement.

He folded his arms across his chest, excited to hear 'her' idea.

Her green eyes sparkled as she enthused about going away with their friends.

He pretended to consider it.

'We should ask Tiana and Lia,' he said.

He liked an entourage and Lia and Tiana were particularly attentive. Loyal hounds, he liked to think. He only had to alternate the smiles with frowns, and they'd be falling over themselves to do whatever he wanted.

'What about you? Aren't you bringing anyone?'

'I'll ask Hugo.'

He hadn't quite finished exhorting money from his wealthy friend, and besides, he might need a wingman.

Willow pulled a face. 'If you have to. Maybe I should invite Spence too?'

His smile wilted. 'You think you'll still be seeing him, then?'

'Of course I will. Why not?'

His gaze met hers. 'It's a risk. That's all I'm saying. Besides, you'd be the only couple. Are you sure you want to be stuck entertaining your boyfriend every single evening, when your friends want to party? Nothing against Spence, but he doesn't strike me as the party type.'

Willow faltered. He could see he had planted the seed of doubt in her mind.

'Anyway, up to you.'

He would leave it in her hands. If Spence did come, there were ways of dealing with him. There was a certain lawlessness when you went on holiday to a foreign country. No one knew quite how things operated. People let their guard down, dazzled by the sun. Josh could do pretty much what he wanted and no one would suspect.

'What about Mum?' Willow said, shaking him out of his reverie.

'What about her?'

'Well, you know. She's going to have kittens when we tell her we want to go away without her. She's going to take some convincing.'

'We're adults. She can't stop us.'

A little smirk played on Willow's lips. 'Well, technically, I'm an adult. You're still a kid till August.'

'Piss off.'

'Just saying.'

He let her get away with it, just as he always did. It would wait. It could always wait. His revenge would be so much sweeter.

'We'll talk to Mum together,' he said. 'Make it sound like we're asking her advice. Asking, not telling. She'll like that. Make her feel like part of the decision.'

Willow tilted her head. 'I like that. You're not just a pretty face.' She turned towards the door, then looked back at him. 'You are mostly a pretty face. You shouldn't use so much tinted moisturiser. You look kind of metro.'

'I'm cool with that.'

'I bet you are.'

His ploy worked. Their mother wasn't pleased when they approached her. She wore her anxiety in her shoulders, but she was careful not to freak. She, too, knew how to play the game.

After she had given her assent, Willow scuttled back to her room to call Tiana and Lia. Josh hadn't even bothered to ask Hugo yet. He didn't need to. He would tell Hugo what they were doing and Hugo would say 'yes.' That was how it worked between them.

Back in his room, he logged into his mum's Facebook account to check her private messages. He made it his habit to check in on her. He had been doing it since he was nine. He wasn't a fan of surprises. He liked to know what she was thinking, and fortunately, women of her generation thought nothing of putting all their thoughts into a private message.

He discovered she'd been communicating with a woman called Kelly. His eyes flicked across the screen, widening in anger and disbelief. It would appear Kelly was planning to spy on him and Willow in return for payment. Quite an enterprising idea. He should have been shocked his mother had agreed to it. But he wasn't. This was exactly who Patsy was. She couldn't let them go, could she? He was practically an adult, and she still thought she could run his life.

Wow, wow, wow, he thought. *You've really crossed a line this time.*

I'm going to have to teach you a lesson.

CHAPTER FORTY
JOSH

Two Weeks Earlier

He had hated his family for a long time. Hated being the only male in the house. Years of enduring girly stuff. Being mothered by both his mother and his sister. Being emasculated. Patronised.

They had no idea who he really was. He had a huge following online. Thousands of women flocking to sell his VivaLux products. It was such a simple business idea. He bought up large quantities of cheap or unwanted cosmetics and repackaged them as his own. He would take anything, from perfumes to lip sticks, anti-wrinkle creams and bikini waxes. He didn't care where they came from, how out of date they were, or whether they were tested on animals. He didn't query the ingredients. He ignored reports that showed traces of rat droppings, urine, arsenic or formaldehyde. He repackaged it all and got his beauty consultants to flog it. Some of those women were amazing. They could sell shampoo to baldies. His business had broken even in its first year and then gone from strength to strength. He was now sitting on a small fortune. Enough money to live the life he'd always dreamed of, and Paradise Palms was going to be the perfect place to start.

At the airport, it soon became apparent that Willow thought she was in charge of the trip.

It started when she interrupted his interaction with an attractive girl who wanted help with her suitcase. Willow seemed to think she was a danger to him. What a joke. He had been planning to sign her up to work for him. It never hurt to add new consultants to his list, and this girl looked just the type. Vain and pretty, into her social media. She would have probably been a good seller, and even if she wasn't, she would have bought the cosmetics package every month, just so as not to lose her position on the ladder. They were all so obsessed with their status. It was hilarious.

Now Willow had ruined his approach, he had to pick another target. Women his mum's age were usually good, always looking for a side hustle.

Willow was rolling her eyes, making a big deal out of his supposed naivete. He ought to have slugged her one, but instead, he gave her a cheeky smile.

He was charming, affable. That was his persona. Everybody loved him, even people who barely knew him. Even the customs woman broke into a flustered smile when he looked her way. He went undetected, under the radar, and that was how he liked it. He was the greatest actor of all time, and no one even knew his name.

The villa was a total letdown. A musty odour hung in the air, assaulting his senses as he stepped inside. And his bed was far too small. How could he stretch out on this tiny thing? As for the sheets, way too scratchy. Never mind, it was just a few days. He had been counting down until his eighteenth birthday. Then he would begin living his best life, calling all the shots. Having fun.

He walked over to the balcony and peered down into the water below. It looked even deeper than it had online. He had done his research on this place. It was far more interesting than revising for his tedious exams. He had been fascinated to discover that a young man had fallen from this very balcony and drowned ten years before. So fascinated that he had specifically requested this particular villa.

The rail had looked to be on the low side in the newspaper pictures, and looking at it now, he could see that it was.

'Someone could really hurt themselves,' he said to himself with a smile.

He checked out the cleaning supplies and was pleased to find a tub of wax polish. The lid came off with a satisfying pop, and he breathed in the soothing scent of lavender. Then he checked to see what the others were doing. Spence and Willow were in the kitchen, snogging. It was like watching a dog dismember a carcass. Still, at least it meant they were occupied.

He slipped into their room and spread a generous amount of wax on their balcony floor. It was now as slick as an ice-rink. He was fascinated to see which one of them would skid on it. If he had to guess, Spence would be the most likely victim. With those long limbs, it wouldn't take much to bring him down.

As it turned out, it was Tiana who took the plunge, and unfortunately Josh wasn't around to see it. He was highly annoyed about that, but he didn't want to push his luck. He couldn't arrange two accidents in the same way. Never mind, he had plenty more ideas. He was a creative genius, after all.

If he despised the villa, he loved the resort. He enjoyed everything; the heat of the sun, the coolness of the pool. Not being asked every five minutes if he was old enough to drink. He was sick of having to get his sister to buy all his booze for him because she was already eighteen and he wasn't.

Here, nobody questioned him. It was bliss. He went a bit crazy at first, especially on the boy's night out. He heard Spence on the phone, telling Willow they were being sensible and wouldn't drink too much. Then he put down the phone and ordered a rack of twelve shots. Goodness knows what was in them. They came in a variety of bright unnatural colours and smelt not unlike cleaning fluid. They downed them one after another, the liquid burning the back of their throats, and chased them down with frothy pints of beer. Hugo was already throwing up before they'd even made it back to the villa.

Predictably, Willow slipped into her mum routine, treating him like an irresponsible child. He didn't see the need to go to the hospital, but she was always one to overreact. Besides, he couldn't resist the chance to ogle the nurses. He loved a woman in uniform.

While they sat in the waiting room, he had a word with her.

'Don't tell Mum about this, will you? Or about Tiana's accident.'

'Of course not. What do you take me for?' Willow said a little crossly. 'She'll never let us go on holiday again.'

'As if she has a choice,' he couldn't help saying.

Willow looked at him. 'I know, but we don't want her worrying, do we?'

He looked down at his knees, then he looked up and tried to make his expression mirror hers.

'Poor Mum.'

Had he got it right? He was never quite sure what his face was doing. He pulled out his phone and looked at the camera app to check. He had thought he was doing his sympathetic expression, but when he looked at his reflection, he saw that he was actually smirking. He straightened his lips. He was usually more careful, but sometimes, when he drank alcohol, his mask slipped. And he couldn't have that, could he?

THE KITESURFING ACCIDENT had been all Hugo's idea.

Well, perhaps not directly. But kitesurfing had never even entered Josh's head when he came up with the trip to Bulgaria. He had no plans to harm Hugo until he caught him eyeing up his sister. It was weird, the violent, twisting sensation he felt in his stomach when he spotted it. Willow had already been dating Spence for months. But there was something gross about the idea that Hugo was into her, and it surprised him that Hugo might have an ulterior motive for being his friend. Did he really like Josh, or was he simply using him to get in his sister's pants? Josh wasn't about to find out. So he was more than ready to offer a helping hand when Hugo got ready for his kitesurfing session.

He put his hand in his pocket and smiled when he felt the metal cover of his penknife. Hugo continued to chatter as they set up his kiteboard. It wasn't hard to distract him while he snagged a couple of the strings. Not quite cutting them, but fraying them enough to make them loose. He thought it would be interesting to see what happened if the equipment broke mid air. Hugo would probably fall into the sea, or maybe he would land on someone. Now that would be funny. The anticipation made him want to hug himself as he returned to his sun lounger, but he knew better than to show any emotion. Instead, he sat silently and watched the horizon.

While he was waiting, a girl in a white bikini caught his eye. Her long black hair cascaded down her back and her brown eyes sparkled in the sunlight. He waited for her to notice him, but she walked right by. Unbelievable!

He turned his attention back to Hugo. He looked like he was in trouble up there. His arms and legs were flailing. The kite board was moving at a strange angle. Like it was falling out of the sky. It was! His heart beat faster as it pitched right into the side of a building with a resounding thud.

Wow!

'Oh hell! Is your friend alright?' It was the girl's friend who had spoken, but he looked right through her because the beautiful girl was finally looking at him.

He forced his face to take on an appropriate expression. How should he be feeling right now? Sad? Concerned?

Willow was already running towards Hugo. Willow to the rescue! She should be a doctor, he sometimes thought. The way she was always running to help people. It was as if she was forever trying to make up for not saving their father. They never talked about that day, the two of them. He wasn't even sure she remembered. Josh had seen his father tumble down the stairs, tripping over their toys as he went.

'You can't call for an ambulance,' he had told her. 'We're going to get in trouble.'

'But we need a doctor!'

'It's all your fault!' he had told her. In that moment, he had really thought it was. Those were Willow's marbles, scattered all over the stairs. It didn't matter that they'd both been playing with them.

'If you call for help, they'll take him away.'

He had been right about that part. When their mum finally came home, their father *was* taken away, never to be seen again, and nothing was ever the same again.

HUGO'S FACE was doing some weird thing. He kept opening and closing his mouth. Was he in pain? Everyone around him looked alarmed. Josh ambled over, but was told to stand clear.

Hugo was clutching Willow's hand. Oof! Spence would hate that.

'Not much room in that ambulance,' he commented casually. 'Looks a bit of a squeeze.'

Spence frowned, but he didn't interfere. How could he? Hugo was hurt. He sat down on the sand and pulled out his little red book. He was composing a poem, Josh realised. How pathetic. Feeling restless, he started to walk back down towards the sea where Tiana and Lia were prancing about in the waves.

'Hey!' he turned and saw the beautiful girl standing behind him. She spoke through her hand, as if she didn't want anyone to hear her.

He took a step towards her. 'Are you talking to me?'

'Do you see anyone else worth talking to?'

He erupted with laughter. 'No, I suppose not.'

'What do you think you're doing on my beach?'

'Your beach?' He looked around in amusement. 'You own it, do you?'

She kept her voice low. 'In the winter, nobody comes here but me. I like to swim out to that rock over there.'

She pointed to a spot way out on the horizon.

'I swim out there and look out to sea. Once in a while I see a boat, but mostly, it's just me.'

'It must be cold in the winter.'

'It is so cold, my entire body turns numb. Sometimes I don't know if I'm going to make it back to the shore, but I always do.'

'Next, you're going to tell me you sit on the rocks and lure sailors with your songs.'

'I could if I wanted to.' She glanced left and right. 'Today, there are too many tourists. They clutter the place up like filthy seagulls. Do you want to get out of here?'

'Okay. Why are we whispering?'

'My parents are very strict. They don't allow me to date.'

He nodded. He liked that. It would be fun to sneak around behind their backs.

He allowed himself a longer glance. This girl was not just pretty, she was stunning, and yet there was a wolfishness to her smile.

'Why don't you walk a bit ahead of me?' he said. 'Take me somewhere quiet, where we can be alone.'

He headed back to his deckchair and gathered up his stuff.

'Still got a bit of a headache.' he told Spence. 'I'm going to head back to the villa.'

Spence nodded.

Tiana appeared in front of him. 'You're leaving already?'

'I'll rest up, and then I will be back to my usual entertaining self by dinner.'

She nodded, hanging on his every word. She was quite attractive, Tiana. Shame she was so easy. There was no fun there. No chase.

The beautiful girl slipped on a pair of white shorts and a floaty white top that fluttered in the breeze. She headed for the path that led to the cliffs, her long hair trailing behind her like ribbons. He glanced around to make sure no one was watching, then he followed.

She was so graceful, the way she moved. She reminded him of a butterfly. She led him on quite a hike up the cliffs. The path went on for ages, taking him round bends and twists. Finally, she brought him to an old lookout hut. The place was already equipped with a thin mattress and covered with a blanket. He guessed they weren't the first teenagers to use the space for this purpose. She laid down and looked up at him. Her smile was radiant and inviting. He gazed into her eyes and had a strange realisation that she wasn't like all the other girls he had dated. There was something special about this one. He wanted to keep her.

CHAPTER FORTY-ONE
JOSH

After Willow, Tiana, and Lia left for Sozapol, he headed to Kelly's kiosk and bought some pastries and a bottle of coke. As she handed him his change, he noticed a shadow pass over her face, and sensed the unease in her posture. There was definitely something off about her. A darkness he couldn't identify. Her interest in him and his friends was unnatural. He knew she had offered to spy on them for his mum, but she seemed genuinely fascinated. Obsessed, even. She was constantly watching them. And yet she didn't appear to be reporting much to his mother. He had checked her messages, and they were all superficial and uninformative. No mention of the alcohol poisoning they'd suffered, or any of the accidents. She was feeding Patsy a fantasy.

'Off somewhere nice?' she asked.

'Just thought I'd explore the town a bit,' he said vaguely.

'Oh. Well, the market's on today.'

'Great.'

He shot her a winning smile, but he didn't give a fart about the market.

He had ordered himself a taxi, but he didn't want anyone

to see it picking him up. As he waited at the agreed pick up point, he spotted a figure coming out of one of the houses. His heart leapt as he realised it was Elizaveta. Her long hair was bundled up on top of her head and she was carrying a broom and a bag of cleaning products.

He ran down the road towards her, surprised at his own delight in spotting her unexpectedly like this.

'Elizaveta!'

'Josh!'

She glanced quickly around, but there didn't appear to be anyone about.

They stood awkwardly on the path, her still clutching her broom.

'What are you doing here?' she said. 'You know we can't be seen together.'

'I was just passing when I spotted you.'

'And I am going to work.'

He cleared his throat. It was so important that he make a good impression on her, that he let her know he was worth her time.

'Listen, I had a great time with you yesterday. I don't normally do this, but is there any chance I can see you again?'

She looked at him doubtfully. 'I don't know about that. You know my parents don't want me to have a boyfriend, and besides, you will be going home soon.'

He drew a breath. 'What if I told you I'm not going home? I have something much more exciting planned.'

'Like what?'

'I'm going to travel the world.'

She laughed. 'How do you plan to do that? You don't even have a car.'

'No, I have something better.'

'What's that?'

'A boat.'

'What kind of boat?'

'A good one. Actually, I'd say it's more of a yacht.'
'You're lying.'
'I can show you tonight if you want?'
'Is this some kind of joke?'
'I'm serious. Come down to the harbour at eight o'clock and you can meet the real me.'
'Well, now, I have to ask. Who is the real you, Josh?'
'Someone who knows what he wants and goes after it, and to hell with the consequences.'
She had a playful glint in her eye. 'That sounds both fascinating and a little dangerous.'
'Life is too short to play it safe.'
'Well, I suppose some risks are worth taking.'
'Like me, you mean?'
'Are you a risk to me, Josh?'
'Always.'

He leaned in and his lips brushed hers, the slightest touch sending a spark of electricity shooting through his body. But it wasn't only her who was in danger here, he realised. He was really falling for her, and he wasn't sure what to do about it. This wasn't part of his plan, but he couldn't stop himself from wanting her more fiercely with every passing second.

HE FEIGNED sleep all the way to Sozopol, so the taxi driver couldn't draw him into conversation. As soon as he arrived, he headed into the toilets to put on his disguise. He pulled his baseball cap down and slid on shades to hide his forehead and a fake beard to hide his chin.

Next, he looked around for a car that would be easy to start. Stealing cars was a skill he had learned at a young age, thanks to a friend's father. Ron had taught him the basics. The trouble was, there were so many newer cars out now, and some of them proved more challenging with their advanced security systems.

He scanned the rows of cars parked haphazardly along the side of the street. His eyes landed on a faded black Toyota with rusted fenders and a dented bumper. The window was already half wound down, making his job easy. No one took any notice as he reached in and opened the door. He had no trouble getting it started, though driving it was another matter. He had never driven on the right before. He kept drifting into the middle of the road, then he would remember and swerve back into his lane.

He cruised through the town until he caught sight of Tiana's bright pink skirt. She and the others were just leaving a restaurant and heading towards the beach. A mischievous grin spread across his face as he followed them. He enjoyed people watching. It was always interesting, like watching animals at the zoo. He hoped they wouldn't be too long, because he couldn't hold onto this car forever.

He must have fallen asleep in the heat. Not surprising, given that the car had lousy air conditioning. He sat up and peered over the wheel. Through bleary eyes, he saw the girls emerge from the beach, talking and giggling.

His eyes were fixated on Willow, who was lagging slightly behind the group. He started the engine and followed them slowly. He let them walk back down the road towards the bus stop. It was quiet there. He didn't want any witnesses. Not if he was going to take Willow out.

He went for it, putting his foot on the accelerator as he sped towards them. At the last minute, Lia stepped out onto the road and got in the way. Instinctively, he swerved, hitting the bin, and sending Lia flying.

God dammit. Trust Lia to screw this up for him.

. . .

The Beach

He went round again, passing them slowly as they stood by the bus stop. He thought about making a second attempt, but there were too many other people now. He didn't need half a dozen witnesses snitching to the police.

He got a good look at them. Willow was chewing her hair, which meant she was stressed. Her eyes darted about, like she knew he was watching her. He was surprised she didn't spot him.

He thought about driving the car back to Paradise Palms, but it was a temperamental motor, and he knew that the longer he had it, the greater the chance that the police would pick him up. In the end, he ditched it outside a motel and walked down the street to hail a taxi. It wasn't hard. They always stopped for him.

The taxi brought him down to the harbour, where his boat, The Magnificence, was waiting. Its white hull sparkled in the golden light. He walked towards it, eager to inspect the vessel that would be his home for the next few months. It was medium-sized, sleek, and elegant. The crew stood by, ready to assist him. Their English was limited, but he wasn't hiring them for their conversation. As long as they could cook, clean and steer, that was all he needed. That and their total discretion.

The interior surpassed his expectations. He had a large bedroom with shiny satin sheets and a bottle of champagne waiting for him on ice. A smile played on his lips as he imagined bringing Elizaveta here tonight. He couldn't wait to give her a taste of the luxurious lifestyle he could provide.

His phone beeped. Willow wanted to know where he was. He couldn't be bothered to reply. He was still annoyed that he had gone all the way to Sozapol, only to be cheated out of a cool hit. Never mind, Elizaveta would be here soon. She would brighten his mood.

While he had been in Sozapol, Elizaveta had been working all day, cleaning hotel rooms. He didn't like the thought of her working like a servant. She was like Cinderella, waiting for her Prince Charming. Well, he would certainly rise to the role.

Eight o'clock, he had told her. Now it was nearly nine. He had never waited for any girl before. He was usually the one who kept them waiting. But the dynamic with Elizaveta was different. He wanted her so much it made him queasy.

Finally, she appeared, her long crimson dress blazing behind her like a trail of fire, and instantly he forgave her. She sashayed up the gangway and he helped her step onboard, the soft fabric of her dress shimmering under the lights.

He brought her into the dining room, where they ate oysters that melted in their mouths, smoked salmon canapes and tiny duck tarts. The music in his head was deep and intoxicating.

Later, they stepped out onto the deck, and he immediately felt the vast expanse of the night sky. A deep indigo hue spread out before them, sprinkled with countless stars that glittered like diamonds against a velvet backdrop. The gentle lapping of the waves echoed in his ears, filling him with a sense of tranquillity. In that moment, it was as if they were the only two people in the entire world.

'For so long, I've felt like a prisoner in my own life,' he said. 'Going through the motions, following the rules. But all this time, I've been waiting for my life to begin, and now that I've met you, I'm beginning to understand what I've been missing.'

She gazed into his eyes and he was struck by their depth and beauty. Every time he blinked, it was like emerging from an abyss, only to be pulled back by her alluring gaze. He feared that if he wasn't careful, he would drown in those deep, dark pools.

'I should get home now,' she said as he uncorked a fresh bottle of champagne. 'I need to be up early to do my chores.'

The smile froze on his lips. 'How about you don't go home?' He kept his voice low and seductive. 'How about you stay here and be my wife?'

Before she could even answer, he signalled his crew to start the engine. Darkness enveloped them as they headed out to sea.

CHAPTER FORTY-TWO
JOSH

The boat rocked as it sliced through the pitch-black water, leaving the lights of the land behind. Elizaveta's fingers clenched the rail, her eyes wide with fear. Perhaps she was beginning to tune into his true nature, and sensed his marriage proposal was not optional. He felt the darkness creeping closer, seeping into every corner of his being.

She swallowed hard. 'I will marry you, Josh. But first you have to take me home.'

'No way.' He shook his head. 'Your parents will never allow it.'

'They might. Given time.'

No. He had done his research, and he knew enough to know that they would not give in so easily.

'Please, Josh. I want to say goodbye to my life here. I need to pack up some of my things, spend a little time with my friends and family. Give me a few days. I'll be back, I promise. You know how I feel about you.'

He hesitated. There was a strong chance she wouldn't return, and yet it would be so much easier if she came willingly. Maybe it was worth the risk?

'You can't tell anyone,' he said. 'They will spoil it.'
She nodded. 'I won't tell a soul.'
'I'm not going back to my old life. Do you understand? They'll be looking for me. My sister will report me missing. The police might even ask you questions.'
'And I will tell them I don't know you. We barely even met. No one can dispute that. No one's seen us together. We've been so careful.'
He looked deep into her eyes, breathed in her scent, and released his grip. This must be what true love felt like.
With a flick of his hand, the boat turned around, gliding smoothly through the water. He helped her disembark, her feet barely touching the deck, before she scurried off to her house, her silhouette disappearing into the darkness.
The moonlight danced on the ripples of the water, casting a surreal glow over his world. He toyed with the idea of returning to the villa, to his friends and his sister, but he couldn't bear the suffocating feeling that came over him when he was around them.
Tomorrow would be his birthday, and Willow had arranged a lame party for him. She had been going on about it all week, and it sounded increasingly tedious the more she mentioned it. It had never occurred to her to ask him what he wanted. She liked getting dressed up and sitting in stuffy restaurants, so that was what she had planned. It hadn't occurred to her that he'd prefer to go bungee jumping, or exploring the caves. He yearned to leave them all behind and begin anew. His impatience grew as he waited for Elizaveta's return.
Until she came back, he couldn't be sure of her love for him, a thought that made his heart ache in an unfamiliar way. This dependence on someone else was a foreign feeling for him, one that he didn't enjoy. It was both exhilarating and terrifying at the same time.
His knuckles turned white as he clenched his fists, his

anger and frustration boiling beneath the surface. Elizaveta had better return, or her whole family would pay.

CHAPTER FORTY-THREE
JOSH

Josh lay in the small, cosy cabin, enjoying the silence that was only broken by the soothing lull of the waves against the hull. The rhythmic sound calmed his mind and body. Without Hugo's infernal snoring, he had slept like a baby, but as he stretched out his hand, he couldn't help but feel the absence of Elizaveta's warm presence beside him. In such a short time, she had become essential to him, like oxygen for his soul, and her absence left an ache in his chest. He reached for his business phone, hoping for a message from her, but there was none. He replayed the moment he had asked her to marry him, trying to decipher her expression. Was she genuinely interested in spending her life with him? Or had she run for the hills?

He had intended to stay on the boat. He didn't want to be spotted around town now that it was time to disappear. And yet his heart raced with anxiety about Elizaveta. She made it impossible to think clearly. He stood on the deck. The salty sea air whipped against his face and tangled his hair. Elizaveta had bewitched him.

He could barely stomach his breakfast, the fine food sticking to his throat like glue, and when he opened his laptop, his thoughts were too scattered to focus on work, even though his accounts revealed that he had increased his profits overnight. But he couldn't enjoy it. Not until he knew for sure if Elizaveta would be coming back.

Distracted, he unzipped his bag of disguises and selected a greying beard. He added a thick moustache to complete the look, along with a pair of plain glasses and a simple hat.

Satisfied with his transformation, he set off into town, blending seamlessly with the tourists. His old phone let out a small beep and he checked the screen. The message was from Willow. She was worried because he hadn't been home the night before. He smirked as he pictured her anguish. She would probably be having kittens. Willow did not like feeling out of control. She needed everything to go her way. Well, the power dynamic between them had shifted. He pictured the fire in her eyes. She had no idea what was to come.

Seagulls squawked overhead as he hiked up the cliff path. As he reached the hideout, he paused to take in the awe-inspiring view of the jagged cliffs below. He looked down and saw his boat. It looked like a tiny toy against the vastness of the sea. He loved it up here. There was freedom in the stillness, the silence. Standing on the edge, with no railings or barriers, he felt both exhilarated and terrified at the sheer drop. It was like standing on the edge of the world.

He didn't meet a soul as he hiked back down. But as he took the track that led back towards the town, he had a creepy feeling down his spine. As if someone or something was watching him. He whirled round, but there was no sign of anyone. He couldn't tell if the feeling was real, or if he was being paranoid. Hadn't Willow mentioned exactly the same thing?

He crossed the field that led to the back of Elizaveta's house. As he reached her garden, clusters of delicate five-petaled periwinkles swayed gently in the warm breeze, their sweet aroma filling his senses. He texted her, but she did not reply. White hot anger sparked within him. Was she intentionally ignoring him? His phone pinged.

Where are you?

He stared at it for a minute, not understanding. Then he realised it was from Willow. Of course. Today was his birthday. She would be expecting to see him, to skim the cream from the day so that all he was left with was the milk. She had a way of doing that, Willow. She would smile and clap and make out that she was happy for him to take his moment in the limelight, but then he would look at her unexpectedly and find her scowling, unhappy that it was his moment and not hers. The jealousy of siblings was always there, bubbling under the surface. Even now they were supposedly grown up.

He crouched in the shadows outside Elizaveta's house. As the lights flickered off, he scanned the walls for a way to scale up to her room. A twisted thought crossed his mind as he imagined her letting down her hair, like Rapunzel. But of course that was nonsense - if he were to use her hair as a rope, it would rip from her scalp, and her blood would rain down all over his face.

He discovered an old wooden ladder in her neighbour's outbuilding and dragged it across the garden, leaning it up against her window. The ladder trembled beneath his weight and he was about half way up when he realised some of the rungs were rotten. But he could hear Elizaveta's voice. Her laughter. It was tantalising. Who did she have up there? He had to see.

His hands gripped the rough edges of the windowsill, his biceps and forearms straining with the effort. Elizaveta was not alone. She had three friends with her. They were watching TV and bashing each other with pillows. This was clearly a sleepover. A farewell party, he hoped.

He thought about banging on the window and gatecrashing their evening, but he had a feeling Elizaveta wouldn't like that. And he wanted so badly for her to leave with him. He would have to be patient. What was a couple more nights?

Dejected, he climbed back down the ladder, dragged it back to the neighbour's house and headed back to the boat, where he spent the night of his eighteenth birthday alone.

The following day, there was a buzz about him online. He read the news with excitement.

People were talking about him. He was officially missing.

The early editions of the local news carried his picture, although not as prominently as he might have liked. He wasn't a missing woman, after all. Willow had chosen a particularly ugly picture of him to give to the press. Knowing her, she had done so intentionally, to spite him for disappearing.

By now he had disposed of his old phone and switched entirely to his business one. He didn't need to read Willow's pathetic messages to know that the search for him was heating up.

He itched to head over to the kiosk, where all the search teams were gathering. He could picture himself joining one, helping with the search. People were so stupid, nobody would even realise.

He was watching when Willow and Spence appeared, flanked by a group of volunteers. It looked like they had the dregs of the search teams. These people all looked like tourists, and some of them were clearly unfit, stumbling and panting as they headed up the cliff path. He saluted them from the deck of his boat.

Good luck, team. You're going to need it!

What were they doing up there anyway? He grimaced at the thought of those people stumbling on his secret hideout. Had he left any traces of himself there? He didn't think so.

After an hour or so, several members of the search team headed back down, shoulders slumped in defeat. He counted six of them. That just left Willow and Spence. He smiled slowly. Perhaps he should go and give them a helping hand.

He put on a long, frizzy wig and stuck a hat over the top, then added sunglasses.

He started up the cliff path, taking the most direct route. It wasn't the easiest climb, but having done it a few times now, he had an advantage. He hiked along until he heard Willow and Spence. The sound of their bickering voices echoed off the surrounding rocks. Sounded like trouble in paradise. Willow forged ahead, leaving Spence to drag his feet.

It was so secluded up here that he could no longer control his impulses. At one point, Spence stopped and stared down at the sea below him. He was very close to the edge. Definitely closer than was advisable. The jagged cliffs loomed below him, their sharp edges cutting into the vast expanse of blue sky.

Josh crept closer. Maybe his footsteps were too loud, or perhaps he just sensed the tension in the air, but at the very last minute, Spence whirled round. His jaw dropped, but before he could utter a sound, Josh was hurtling towards him, shoving him as hard as he could. There was a moment when Josh felt himself wobble, but he righted himself just in time to see Spence somersault over the edge, landing on the ledge below with an almighty crack.

He shook his head in wonder. What a landing! But there was no time to celebrate. Willow would soon realise Spence wasn't behind her. Maybe she had even heard the impact. All around him, birds were taking flight. He took the most direct route, cutting through shrubbery to scramble back down the cliffs. Then he heard a noise like an animal howling. Except it was Willow, crying for her lost love.

He hid behind a bush until it was safe and headed back to the harbour. A helicopter hovered overhead, pulling Spence up into the sky. He watched with fascination, picturing what would happen if he fell from that height, his body exploding as he hit the sea. Spence was pulled safely inside, and then the helicopter moved off again, buzzing away like a giant damselfly. Josh gave it a little wave. His heart jumped as he spotted The Magnificence waiting for him at the end of the pier. He hurried towards it, right past Willow, who was too busy blubbering to notice him. He kept on going, and didn't look back. And when he finally reached the boat, there was Elizaveta waiting for him.

CHAPTER FORTY-FOUR
JOSH

There was a flurry of messages back and forth between his mother and Willow. Then they stopped. He gathered that meant Patsy was flying out, but the only way he could know for sure was to send Elizaveta out to spy. Better her than him, because while he could fool the rest of the world, his own mother would know him no matter how good a disguise he wore. Much as he wanted to be the one to seal her fate, he was going to need Elizaveta's help.

'But why?' she asked, when he explained what he wanted her to do.

'Because they will never let me lead the life I want. Living with them was pure torture. It's time to break free.'

Getting rid of Willow would be especially satisfying. Having spent a lifetime in her shadow, it felt amazing to know that next year, he would grow older than her. He knew how much she would hate that, probably even more than the fact that he had killed her.

As for his mum, he might have let her live if it weren't for the fact that she had hired Kelly to spy on him. The idiocy of the woman. Kelly could be anyone. She could be a raving psychopath, for all she knew. It was a monumental mistake, and she couldn't be allowed to get away with it.

Once Elizaveta had helped lure his mother and sister into the shipping container, he took great pleasure in locking the door after them. He had done his research. This particular consignment was due to set sail in less than an hour. Soon, they would be gone forever.

He headed back to his own boat and watched as the larger vessel headed off through the shimmering blue waters. A rush of exhilaration coursed through his veins as he watched it disappear over the horizon. His new life was just beginning. A perfect life, away from the suffocating demands of his family. He turned to Elizaveta and swept her up into his arms.

'Where do you want to go first?' he asked.

Elizaveta didn't have to think about it. 'Morrocco. I've always wanted to go there.'

'Morrocco it is,' he said with a smile.

He leaned back and clicked his fingers. Instantly, one of the crew brought over a bottle of champagne and filled two flutes. They clinked glasses and gazed out to sea.

Two weeks later, he sat in the dining room across the table from Elizaveta. One of the crew appeared with a menu. Josh pointed at what he wanted, watching the horizon as Elizaveta ordered. They were running low on fresh produce, and the sea was beginning to lose its allure. Whereas in the beginning he enjoyed the gentle motion of the boat, it now grated on him, having to chase things across the table as they slid away.

He perused the wine list, choosing a bold red. The waitress brought it immediately and he took a small sip, unsure if he like the flavour. He reminded himself that he needed to expand his tastes and appreciate the finer things in life.

The Beach

The chef made them lobster bisque, followed by some Bulgarian dish Elizaveta favoured.

As she picked at her food, he noticed worry lines forming on her forehead.

'How are the wedding preparations going?' he asked.

Her smile seemed a little forced. 'I've ordered my dress and a suit for you. We'll pick them up when we reach the port. But Josh, isn't there some way we could invite my mum?'

He stiffened at her words. 'Absolutely not.'

'Please?'

He locked eyes with her across the table, silently begging her to understand. They couldn't risk inviting anyone from their old lives. They needed to remain hidden and start again.

Besides, he didn't like what he had seen of her parents. They worked every day except Sunday, and spent most of their free time in church. And he had thought his mum was dull.

He wanted to show Elizaveta the good life. He thought she understood that.

'My love, you can have any jewellery you desire. Any dress. Any handbag. We'll go to all the best festivals, all the best parties. But we can never go back to our old lives, our old families. I thought you understood that?'

She put down her fork and sat in silence for the rest of the meal. He left her to stew for a while. He was not going to change his mind. She might as well get used to it. Besides, cutting her off from her family would be good for their relationship. It would be easier to control her that way. He didn't want her turning to her mother every time they had a disagreement. Once they were married, she shouldn't need anyone but him.

He sat at his laptop for a while, checking on his various business portfolios. His decision to pull all his money from

VivaLux had been catastrophic for the company, but excellent for him. He now had millions to play with, and better still, he'd never have to work another day in his life.

He stopped a passing member of the crew.

'Where is Elizaveta?'

'In the galley, Sir.'

He nodded and headed for the door that led to the galley kitchen. He discovered her sitting at the table, scribbling furiously.

'What are you doing?'

He read the guilt in her eyes. Her pen dropped to the floor. He tore the letter from her hands.

It was all in Bulgarian. He couldn't read it.

'Who are you writing to?'

She didn't answer.

His chest tightened and he grew more angry.

'Tell me at once, or I'll get someone to translate.'

She met his eye. 'I'm writing to my mum, if you must know. Just to let her know I'm alright.'

The sky darkened. Panic swelled in his chest.

'She'll see the postmark. You'll give us away.'

'She won't come looking for me if she knows I'm safe.'

'She already knows you're safe. You left her a note, remember?'

'I know, but she's my mother. She'll be worried.'

She stood and pushed past him, her long hair cascading down her back. The door slammed behind her. He remained in the kitchen and poured himself a large shot of rum. It tasted sickly sweet, but he craved the warmth it gave him. He wasn't used to a woman who stood up to him, but he wanted her more than ever.

He finished the first drink and poured himself another, hoping it would numb his brain. The door creaked open, and he turned expectantly, only to see the cook's worried eyes. The cook took one look at him and scuttled away like a cockroach.

The Beach

. . .

He downed the rest of his drink and walked around the boat, searching for Elizaveta. He finally found her in the bathroom. She was sitting on the floor, surrounded by her severed locks. A pair of scissors lay discarded behind her, glinting in the light. He swallowed hard. All that beautiful hair. He couldn't believe she had chopped it all off.

'Now you won't want me,' she said, tears streaming down her face. 'Now you'll have to let me go.'

He shook his head, too angry to speak.

'You'd better clear all that away before I come back.'

He left her there and stormed out onto the deck.

The wind howled, and waves crashed against the side of the boat, but he remained out there for hours, paralysed with anger and frustration.

And that was where he remained until the news came in about his mum and Willow. Then his fury knew no bounds.

CHAPTER FORTY-FIVE
JOSH

Now

He paced back and forth on the deck; the rain pelting his face with icy droplets. His heart thumped violently in his chest, matching the rhythm of the raging sea. He wanted to stay out here and let the storm absorb all his anger and pain, but he couldn't control himself any longer. Eighteen years of self control had come undone in a matter of days.

He didn't even notice when Elizaveta emerged from the cabin.

'You should come inside. You're getting soaked.'

He clenched his jaw. 'Have you heard? About my mum and Willow? They've been found alive.'

She stared at him. 'How is this possible?'

He made his way towards her.

'It's all your fault,' he snarled, grabbing her by the shoulders. 'You didn't do your job properly.'

'I did! I did exactly as you said.'

He raised his hand and struck her across the cheek.

'It's all your fault.'

'Josh!'

There was a startled expression on her face.

He grabbed her again, his fingers ripping through the uneven lengths of hair at the back of her head. He had only intended to frighten her, but he couldn't communicate that message to his brain.

'Josh, stop it!'

He tore the thin fabric of her shirt and shoved her away with brute force. A sickening crack echoed through the boat as she hit the deck and blood poured from her head like crimson rain.

Her eyes grew heavy. She stopped fighting against him and lay back in surrender. He knelt down beside her.

'Stop pretending,' he whispered, but there was no response from her lifeless body. She was just a rag doll in his arms.

CHAPTER FORTY-SIX
JOSH

It was dark as Josh arrived at the port. A chill ran down his spine and he wished he had brought his jacket. He turned, expecting Elizaveta to be right behind him, but of course she wasn't. He had thrown her body overboard to the sharks.

He took a slow, faltering step forward. He needed to snap out of it. Mistakes happened. He was going to embrace life, start again. He was too young to settle down, anyway. It was time to party.

The hour was late, but that was fine by him. All the best parties started after midnight. As he stepped into the waiting limo, he was glad of the complimentary drinks on offer and popped one open. The driver pulled away, and he glanced back at the boat, his crew watching him leave.

He sipped his drink and looked out the window, marvelling at how different it was from his preconceived notions of Morocco. Where were the camels? The weather was hot, but not as intense as he had expected. It reminded him of Bulgaria, with its dry heat. The buildings were similar too, the same red-tiled roofs lined the streets. It almost felt like he could be back there, instead of halfway across the world.

The Beach

Then he saw a road sign. It was in Cyrillic.

The driver's gaze flickered to him in the mirror, lingering a little too long for comfort. He shifted in his seat. He knew he was attractive, but he wished she would focus on the road. As he leaned back, exhaustion seeped through his bones. He was having trouble keeping his eyes open. Perhaps he should stop somewhere for a coffee to perk himself up.

As they slowed for the traffic lights, he got a good look at her. There was something strikingly familiar about her. Those crinkly eyes, that crooked nose.

'Hey, do I know you?'

He rattled the door handle, but it was locked.

The lights changed, and the car accelerated way too fast. Panic rose inside him.

'What…what's happening?'

Kelly met his eye in the mirror. 'I promised your mother I'd keep an eye on you, and I'm a woman of my word.'

AUTHOR'S CORNER

Dear Reader,

As you turn the final page, I want to extend a heartfelt thanks for joining me on this journey. I hope you enjoyed diving into the world of *The Beach*. Patsy's decision to hire Kelly to watch over her children in Paradise Palms was undoubtedly a controversial one, but it came from a deep place of love and concern. Having lost her husband when the children were very young, Patsy felt an overwhelming responsibility to protect them no matter what. In hiring Kelly, she truly believed she was making the best choice for their safety.

Patsy's overprotectiveness also influenced Willow. For her, the holiday was a crucial step into adulthood, and a chance to prove she was ready to be more independent. When Spence decided to gatecrash, it really threw her for a loop. How could she stand on her own two feet whilst having to deal with his jealousy and clinginess the whole time?

Neither Patsy nor Willow fully grasped the impact of Bill's death on Josh. Both siblings struggled with their loss, but Josh, as the only male left in the family, took it particularly badly.

Not only did he blame Willow for their father's death, but he felt also suffocated by his mother and sister. This resentment simmered throughout his childhood, and as he entered his teenage years, it only intensified. In his troubled mind, he found his mother and sister's protective instincts emasculating, leading him to harbour dangerous thoughts of revenge.

If *The Beach* resonated with you, I would be immensely grateful if you could leave a review. Your feedback not only encourages me to keep writing, but also helps other readers discover my work.

To stay updated on new releases, consider joining my Reader's Club at **lornadounaeva.com**

I love hearing what you liked and didn't like about my books, and what else you're currently reading. I'm a sucker for pet pictures too, so please send me those!

Thank you once again for your support. I look forward to sharing more stories with you soon!

Warmest regards,

Lorna

ABOUT THE AUTHOR

Lorna Dounaeva is a politics graduate who worked for the British Home Office before turning to crime fiction. She writes dark domestic thrillers and is especially fond of female villains. She lives in the Orkney islands with her Ukrainian husband and his parents, three children, a crafty cat and a happy dog.

ALSO BY LORNA DOUNAEVA

The Perfect Housemate
The Wife's Mistake
The Family Trap
The Perfect Family
The Wrong Twin
The Girl in the Woods
The Perfect Girl

The McBride Vendetta Psychological Thriller Series

FRY
Angel Dust
Cold Bath Lane
The Wedding (Short Story)
The Girl Who Caught Fire
The Bitter End

Coming Soon

The Perfect Daughter

Printed in Great Britain
by Amazon